Aaam Patol

W9-BNP-896

Donated by

Agnes G. Hodge
Home & School Association

Sounding OFF

Ted STAUNTON

Red Deer PRESS

Copyright © 2004 Ted Staunton
Published in the United States in 2004
5 4 3 2 1

All rights reserved. No part of this publication may be reproduced, stored in a
retrieval system or transmitted, in any form or by any means, without the prior
written permission of Red Deer Press or, in case of photocopying or other repro-
graphic copying, a licence from Access Copyright (Canadian Copyright Licensing
Agency), 1 Yonge Street, Suite 1900, Toronto, ON M5E 1E5, fax (416) 868-1621.

Northern Lights Young Novels are Published by
Red Deer Press
813 MacKimmie Library Tower
2500 University Drive N.W.
Calgary Alberta Canada T2N 1N4
www.reddeerpress.com

Credits
Edited for the Press by Peter Carver
Copyedited by Jill Fallis
Cover and text design by Erin Woodward
Cover image courtesy Super Stock
Printed and bound in Canada by Friesens for Red Deer Press

Acknowledgments
Financial support provided by the Canada Council, the Department of
Canadian Heritage, the Alberta Foundation for the Arts, a beneficiary of the
Lottery Fund of the Government of Alberta, and the University of Calgary.

THE CANADA COUNCIL | LE CONSEIL DES ARTS
FOR THE ARTS | DU CANADA
SINCE 1957 | DEPUIS 1957

National Library of Canada Cataloguing in Publication
Staunton, Ted, 1956–
Sounding off / Ted Staunton.
ISBN 0-88995-293-0
I. Title.
PS8587.T334S66 2004   jC813'.54   C2004-902728-X

To W. Staunton, son and heir.

With thanks to P. Carver and B. Doyle for inspirational lives and free material.

Chapter

"What zits!"

They were coming back from carrying the amps and the bass drum out to the van.

Sam Foster automatically felt his own face for pimples. So far, it had been that kind of a day. Besides, he was getting so used to having earphones and a crash helmet jammed on his head that he forgot it played tricks with his hearing. It was enough to remember that at six foot two and one hundred and thirty pounds he looked like an overly long T-ball stand. Or an inverted exclamation mark. That was what his sister Robin had said. Robin was a journalism student, and literary.

Sam gave the helmet another fruitless tug as, on his other side, Larry said something that might have been "double trouble" or "bubble bubble." Sam knew it was "hubba hubba." He knew because Larry said it at least once an hour. Larry had gotten the phrase from some ancient sitcom and it meant "girl," or, more precisely, "babe." Which meant that Darryl had probably said, "What's this?" or maybe . . .

Well, never mind. Sure enough, ahead of them a girl—make that a babe—was climbing the one step riser to the stage of the Hope Springs Fall Fair talent show, the same stage that Sam, Darryl, and Larry had just graced as ADHD, their alternative/grunge trio. Their performance was one of many things Sam didn't care to think about right now.

For the moment he didn't have to; the girl was more than enough. He couldn't tell whether she was zit-free, thanks to all the makeup she wore beneath a cowboy hat and a waterfall of black curls, but who cared? The curls cascaded down to a bandanna and fringed vest over a gingham shirt. The shirt was knotted coyly at her bare midriff. Sam gaped as she strode to the microphone in boots and tight white jeans. A country-pop karaoke recording twanged.

Larry groaned something like, "Oh, spare me." The girl began to sing. Beneath his helmet, Sam watched her sway. It didn't matter that the music was country karaoke: not only was this girl hubba-hubba material, she could really sing, which put her light-years ahead of ADHD. And then, as her voice soared to the galvanized limits of the Pumpkin Palace, something like magic happened: she hit a note, an absolutely incandescent note, that homed in like a laser-guided missile in Sam's Death Force II video game. For an instant, Sam felt the helmet vibrate, then loosen, then clamp back to his head before he could react.

As the tune went into its instrumental fade, the girl deftly replaced the microphone on the stand, executed a quick mock curtsey, and skittered off behind the 4-H bulletin board that served as a backstage screen. Sam yanked again at the helmet. Around him he heard the muffled sounds of what, for the talent show, could only be described as tumultuous applause. Even the folks over at the cake bakeoff joined in. It was *Lost* all over again. It was *Lost* plus lifesaving plus music. What more could you ask?

"Madison Dakota, everyone," cried the emcee. There was another burst of approval. Sam gave up on the headgear and joined in.

"I'll be right back," he told Larry and Darryl as they started for the rest of the equipment. First, he had to find that girl.

Chapter

Racing off to find an unknown babe with the unlikely name of Madison Dakota was not Sam Foster's usual style, but then neither was wearing a crash helmet. Sam didn't think any of the things that had happened lately were his style, but he suspected others would disagree: his sister Robin, for one.

At least, he felt, the things were not his fault, especially the helmet. That was Darryl's fault, no matter what Darryl said about the earphones. Given the way his supposed best friend had been acting lately, Sam was in no mood to forgive him either.

It had begun the day before, as everybody walked over to Larry's cousin Doug's friend Norm's place. It was Friday, after school, the end of a second exhausting week in grade nine. Sam was wearing his disc player earphones, a bit of devastatingly subtle reverse psychology to get Steffi Parsons's attention. A lot of people wanted Steffi's attention, including motormouth Darryl. Steffi had returned from a summer out west with aggressively streaked blonde hair and a new outgoingness in areas that until now had been reserved: her chest, for instance. Even Darryl had been reduced to a simple "Holy . . ." on the first day of school.

Unfortunately, apart from time-outs for drooling, that was the last time that Darryl had been speechless around Steffi. He was a one-man wall of noise. Clearly, the countermove was to appear too cool to talk, while not seeming snobby. Steffi, tiring of Darryl, would notice Sam's intriguing reserve. She'd speak to him. He'd play the conversational ace he'd been saving. Result: mutual *Lost* at the very least. Therefore, Sam would be the Serious Drummer of ADHD, studying his craft, ready with a smile or a well-chosen word, but always tuned in to the Beat. Therefore: earphones.

As everyone turned onto Norm's street, Sam's earphones were on, but his CD player wasn't. The batteries had died on the way to school. It didn't matter, as long as he looked good. Besides, he had more than enough to listen to.

". . . the Zipper better than the Octopus. It lasts longer, too." That was Amanda, who was practical, opining to Ashley, Larry, and Delft, the new girl.

"No, no . . . see, the way they rig the ring toss . . ." That was Darryl (who else) in the middle of another endless explanation to Steffi.

"Brrrrrpppppp." That was Steve, to everybody.

The talk was about this weekend's fall fair. In a town the size of Hope Springs, the fair was always a big deal. This year, for Sam, it was bigger than ever. ADHD was in tomorrow's talent show and Sam was helping at the demolition derby. The derby, a contest in which drivers bashed each other's junker cars until only one was left running, was the most popular event at the fair—which said a lot about Hope Springs.

In fact, the derby was why they were all trooping to Norm's: he had a car in the contest. As they covered the last half-block, Sam found himself listening to more than his friends. There were also voices within. *Invite her to the talent contest* and *The derby, the derby!* jostled *You're gonna tank at the contest; just ask her to the fair.* Both were interrupted by *Just keep acting cool. She'll get bored with Darryl and ask you what CD you've got on.*

Sam decided to take this last advice. It was one thing to imagine firing off a well-chosen word; it was another to actually think of one. He spent the final few yards agonizing over what CD he'd claim to be listening to in case Steffi asked. *Lost,* he'd noticed, made decisions difficult.

This was because *Lost* was what you were when you weren't sure about things, like love, for instance. If it wasn't love you were feeling, then it was a simple case of lust, according to something he'd read in a newspaper advice column. Put *love* and *lust* together and you got *Lost,* all the way across town.

Norm's place was a frame bungalow whose front lawn had vanished beneath a triple-wide driveway. An assortment of pickup trucks and small cars with large tires were parked there and on the street. Passing them, Sam saw his chance. As everybody oohed and aahed at the demo derby car and Darryl explained it to the world in general, he'd sidle over to Steffi and sigh, "Sure hope I don't have to push this baby Saturday night." Steffi would say "Whaaaaat?" Sam would shrug and mention that thanks to his friend Smitty, who only organized the whole derby, he was going to be helping out. Steffi would be starry-eyed to learn that Sam was not only a Serious Drummer but also a Guy Who Gets To Stand Around Looking Important In a Day-Glo Vest At The Derby. They'd decide to go to the fair together, leaving Darryl in the dust.

In back of the garage a bunch of guys were gathered around the demo derby car, an ancient Oldsmobile big enough to hold the Fosters' bathroom in its trunk. The guys, clutching beers, were the kind of beefy, capable-looking types that always made Sam feel even gawkier than he was. Instinctively, he went into his Survival Slouch. Even Darryl shut up.

Larry, however, said, "Hey Doug. Hey Norm."

Norm, stylish in oily coveralls and a GM ball cap, nodded. Gangsta rap stuttered from a boom box on the picnic table.

Doug said, "Here to see the Dawg?"

"Oh yeah," Larry said.

The dog? Sam looked around for a pet. Then he saw the doors and hood of the Olds read 99 JUNK YARD DAWG. The white hand-lettering made a tasteful complement to what was left of the original lavender paint job.

"Lookin' good," Larry said appreciatively.

"Effin' right," said Norm, more or less.

Sam guessed it was. With demo derby cars it was hard to tell. The monstrous Olds had clearly taken a few beatings already. For safety, all the glass had been removed and the interior gutted. The doors and trunk were sealed shut; all that remained inside was a driver's seat and a roll cage. A black crash helmet with flame decals lay on the seat.

The group spread out around the car. Darryl was momentarily stuck behind Ashley and Steve. Now was his chance. Sam, still ear-phoned, swallowed hard and eased between Steffi and Delft as an extra trickle of sweat ran down beneath his backpack. He was taking a last, calming breath when Norm levered himself through the driver's side window and turned the key.

The unmuffled Dawg roared to life. Sam jumped. Beneath the testosterone rumble of the V-8 he heard beefy chuckles from Norm and the guys. Face burning, he slouched even more. Norm revved the engine. Sound waves buffeted, the garage window rattled. It was like Steve's burps on steroids. Norm abruptly shut off the engine and looked out.

"Wanna try it?" he said to Steffi. "C'mon, climb in."

Steffi blushed and laughed and shrugged all at once. The boys were helpful with boosts and supporting hands as she clambered through the car window—except for Sam, who opted for more slouching. *Act too cool for this,* came a message from inside. He pretended to adjust his earphones.

"Here, hold this," came a message from outside, specifically from Norm, who was passing the crash helmet out the window as Steffi wiggled herself into the driver's seat. Sam, noticing the wiggling had rucked her T-shirt up above her navel, was too entranced to respond.

Darryl took the helmet. Sam, his eyes still fixed on Steffi's midriff, heard scuffling and giggles and Amanda saying, "Get out, Darryl! Not on me." The next thing he knew something had gripped his scalp, crunching the headphones into his ears.

"Ow! Hey!" He reached up. The crash helmet was jammed on his head. Sam tugged; it was too tight to move. His head had grown along with the rest of him in the last year. "Get it off!"

There was a good deal of distant laughter. Darryl said, "You get it off." His voice seemed to come from somewhere across town.

"I can't. It's stuck." There was more laughter.

"What's goin' on out there?" This from Norm, even farther away.

Amanda appeared. "Bend over," she ordered faintly. There followed a good deal of white noise and discomfort as foam rubber ground against his ears and Amanda and various beefy guys tugged at the helmet. It wouldn't budge.

"Eff, eff, eff," said distant Norm, jackknifing out of the Olds.

"It's his ears. It's stuck on his ears 'cause he's got his headphones on," Darryl explained. "Plus he's got a big head." Sam glared. Darryl's own ears resembled low-flying grapefruit.

He heard Amanda say sarcastically, "Way to go, Darryl," then Norm was grousing about effin' this and effin' that.

Sam couldn't hear what, exactly, but he could guess. He straightened up and through his embarrassment, said the only thing he could think of: "I gotta go."

"Whaddya mean?" demanded Norm. "Where?"

"To work," Sam lied. "But don't worry, I know somebody there who can get it off."

"Well, you effin' better," said Norm. "I need that helmet for tomorrow night."

"I know, I know. Don't worry. Sorry. Gotta go." With a final glare at Darryl, Sam slouched around the corner of the garage. Then he ran.

Chapter

It had not been easy running across town with a pack on his back and a helmet on his head, but it kept Sam ahead of a wave of humiliation and in step with his anger at Darryl. Darryl had been Sam's best friend for what seemed like forever, but in the past few months he had been doing more and more things like, well, this. He'd make plans with Sam, then change his mind when something better came along. He didn't share things anymore. And now, a lot of the time, Darryl's endless explanations sounded as if they were intended to make Sam seem dumb. Which was silly, if you thought about it, because everybody knew Darryl had barely passed grade eight. Sam didn't call himself Albert Einstein, but he knew he could ace Darryl in school any day.

Hope Springs was hilly. Sam was winded in a few blocks, but he pushed on. Smitty was the only person he could think of who could help right now, and he had to get to him before he left J. Earl Goodenough's, where he was supposed to be laying some patio stones in the backyard. Everyone—meaning Steffi—was going to the fair tonight, and Sam didn't plan to be there in a crash helmet.

Downtown, however, he slowed briefly. Racing around there with flames sweeping back where his ears should be might attract more attention than he wanted. Friday afternoons were busy downtown and Lint Lane, a walkway that led from the street to a parking lot, would be filled with skids. As Robin explained it, skids were the older kids at school who made you want to ask, "What did you do that for?" although in nice weather what they mainly did was idle by the pay phone at the entrance to the lane, and snicker at the world.

Sam went into Survival Slouch on the other side of the street, gliding past both the lane and the Bulging Bin, his mom's bulk food store, then taking off again at the end of the block. Downtown Hope Springs was not large.

Loping up the Albert Street hill, he looked anxiously for Smitty's truck. If anybody could pop a helmet off your head, it would be him. Smitty was a family friend, married to Sam's old grade six teacher, Ms. Broom. Sam and Darryl had loved Ms. Broom also, but they had finally accepted that she was attracted to older men, such as ones over twenty. Apart from organizing the demolition derby on behalf of the Yeswecan service club, Smitty (who'd scored a nice win in the lottery a few years back) dabbled in a home maintenance business for older folks around town. Often he passed the Goodenoughs' yard work on to Sam. Stuff that required greater handiness he did himself. Right now, Sam knew, his own head required greater handiness.

Unfortunately, the only person at J. Earl's when he arrived, sweating and breathless, was J. Earl Goodenough himself. The most famous citizen of Hope Springs, J. Earl had written books about all kinds of things. Now semi-retired, the great man spoke his mind twice a week on the national TV news. At the moment he was disconnecting the hose that supplied water to his garden statue. The statue was of a small boy doing what small boys do when they don't wear diapers.

"Why is it that teenage boys never move their arms, no matter how fast they're walking?" J. Earl said by way of greeting. A short, sturdy man with a bald head, his was a voice you heard even with a helmet on. Sam had no time to think of an answer to this, before another question was fired his way: "What the hell have you got on your head?"

This one he could answer. "It's a crash helmet." Sam was used to J. Earl, having once been his paperboy. This and his mom's store had involved them in a number of odd activities, not all of which Sam cared to remember. Of course, this had been when Sam was younger and more prone to silliness.

"I can see it's a crash helmet." J. Earl dropped the hose connection and stood up. "What's it doing there? This a new fashion?"

Sam tried to explain as J. Earl disassembled his spraying statue. The great man growled something in reply. "Pardon?" Sam said.

"I SAID: MAYBE YOU'RE LUCKY IF IT MEANS YOU DON'T HAVE TO LISTEN TO GLEBE."

"Who?"

"GLEBE! WHAT'S THE MATTER WITH YOU, FOSTER— DON'T YOU READ THE PAPER?"

Sam shook his enlarged head. Why would he? The Hope Springs *Eternal* was the most boring reading around, except for his geography textbook. He changed the subject to something more important. "Is Smitty here?"

"Didn't come today." J. Earl's voice subsided as the subject changed. Sam's heart sank. He followed J. Earl as he lugged the base of the statue around into his backyard to the unfinished patio. "The rest of the paving stones didn't come in. Besides, he's busy helping with the fair. Get that other part, would you?"

Sam went back and gingerly picked up the peeing boy. If Smitty was at the fairgrounds already, trying to find him would take forever. He might see him tonight, but Sam needed help before then.

J. Earl put the statue back together as Mrs. Goodenough came outside. She waved to Sam, holding a set of car keys, then came over and said something to J. Earl. He shrugged. Mrs. Goodenough grinned wryly and walked with them to the front yard.

"He's just grumpy because we're going to a party Saturday night."

J. Earl rolled his eyes and stumped into the backyard again, clutching the hose. Sam nodded as if he understood. Why would anyone be upset about going to a party? Then he remembered the fair and Saturday night. Of course. "Too bad you'll miss the demo derby," he said. That would be a disappointment.

Mrs. Goodenough laughed and went to her car. J. Earl called something about the hose. Sam turned on the water tap. Judging by the profanity that suddenly issued from the backyard, it was the wrong thing to do.

"Bend more, or it's going to go all over."

"I'm trying!"

"More!"

Robin's disembodied voice floated above him. Sam craned his neck over the edge of the kitchen table. Now that she went to university and knew everything, his sister had become bossier than ever on her first trip home. Sam found this disappointing. For a while it had seemed that Robin's going away was going to help them get on better. They hadn't argued once in the entire two weeks she'd been away, for example.

"Okay. Now hold still."

Sam tried. It was tough breathing, pressed flat across the table like this. Below him, a copy of the newspaper was spread to catch leakage. At the edges of his vision, he caught glimpses of his parents' feet hurrying back and forth. He could feel the vibration of their steps through the table. Sam wasn't the only Foster caught up by the fair. Mrs. Foster, a member of the fair board, was on duty tonight. Mr. Foster and his Dixieland band (his hobby when he wasn't being a teacher) were performing there tomorrow and he was emcee for this evening's entertainment. Even Robin, sophisticated journalism student that she was, was on her way. She claimed she had to cover it for the *Eternal,* but Sam suspected she was meeting friends and going on the rides.

Still, now that she'd stopped laughing, Robin was the only one who was even trying to help him. His hyper-practical parents, once they found out he wasn't in any great pain or danger, had said they'd deal with it later. Things were just too busy right now. Too busy! Romance with Steffi and revenge on Darryl were hanging in the balance. "Too busy" was pushing it. On the other hand, he hadn't felt like mentioning either of those things to his parents—or Robin.

Now he felt the tug of Robin's fingers on the helmet. He bent his neck further, treating himself to an upside-down underview of the table and chair seats. Then, "AAAGH," he writhed as a chilly stream of olive oil glugged along his neck and in behind his ears.

"Hold still," Robin insisted. "You're going to spill it all over." She poured again. "Now lie there and let it soak in. When it's good and lubricated, I'll get the spatula."

The spatula? Sam lay helplessly, head dangling, and thought dark thoughts about Darryl instead. Why couldn't the guy just give it a rest? It wasn't even as if Darryl was crazy about Steffi. He just wanted everybody to pay attention to him. If everybody—well, the boys, anyway—was paying attention to Steffi, then Darryl wanted some of her spotlight. Sam, *Lost*, knew his own intentions were not as clear-cut.

It could be love he was feeling for Steffi. Still, he suspected it might not be if he ever actually talked to her. Steffi pretty much stuck to a snicker and a "Well, duh" that she delivered with a roll of her made-up eyes. Not that Sam was any talk-show host himself. The conversations he held in the privacy of his own brain sparkled like diamonds. What came out of his mouth generally gleamed like rice pudding.

He sighed. He could feel olive oil oozing through his hair. Drops of it pattered onto the spread-out *Eternal* below. A headline caught his eye:

SUITE SOUNDS FROM GLEBE
Renowned avant-garde composer O. Sidney Glebe
has accepted a commission to create a Hope Springs
Suite, the Friends of Music announced today.

"We're ecstatic," said Friends chair Felice Doberman. "This and the theater restoration will put us on the cultural map."

Mr. Glebe is Canada's best-known contemporary composer, with an international reputation dating back to the 1960s. "Canoe Cantata" and "Aurora Borealis: Orchestral Variations" are among his many works. He will be attending a Friends gala at the home of Mrs. Doberman Saturday evening.

The Hope Springs Suite is expected to premiere sometime next year.

"Hey," Sam said, "I think J. Earl was talking about—"

He raised his head. It was a mistake. Instantly, he felt the olive oil reverse course and run for the back of his neck. "Oh no!" He snatched up the paper to stanch the flow. O. Sidney Glebe and the Hope Springs Suite vanished beneath an oil slick as Robin returned with the spatula.

Chapter 4

The helmet was still in place when Sam, slouching hard, met everyone at the fair gates that night. After a lot of painful tugging and prying, Robin had put down the spatula and announced that he was stuck.

"But I can't go to the fair like this," he'd protested.

"Why not?" Robin had replied. "You don't look much dorkier than usual. Just tell everyone you left your Harley down the street."

His only hope for liberation now was Smitty. Till then, Sam realized as they entered the fairgrounds, if you had to wear dorky headgear, this might be the place to do it. Kids were wearing everything from balloon animals to floppy, red-and-white-striped top hats, all along the midway. And how grumpy could you be as you wandered with your friends, adult-free, through a throbbing paradise of lights, music, and deep-fried onion rings? Rides beckoned, games enticed, riders screamed. Generator cables snaked underfoot. Sam breathed it all in like enriched oxygen. Hope Springs seemed to shrink when you hit fourteen; the fair made it life-sized again.

"It would be cool to burp here," Steve said. They were watching some skids trying to ring a bell with a sledgehammer. Or maybe he said, "work here." Sam was finding hearing even more difficult now that some of the olive oil had gotten in his ears.

"Well, duh," said Steffi.

Amanda said, "Are you kidding? Spend your life in a Porta-Potty?"

"They don't do that. They live in all those RVs and trailers." Darryl gestured beyond the rides. "They're cool. My uncle—"

Sam shut Darryl out by jiggling the now-slippery helmet. Earpiece foam squelched darkly. The neck of his jersey felt oily too. The skid took his last swing with the sledgehammer. The bell didn't ring. The skid's friends laughed. Sam did too. The skid turned. "Hey bowling ball, want me to try it with your head?"

"Effin' niners," said another.

The effin' niners slunk away. Porta-Potties or not, life far from Hope Springs suddenly seemed like a wonderful idea. Sam pictured the open road: cash in your pocket, a cool trailer to live in, no teachers, no homework, late nights, later mornings. Not to mention endless rock and roll (he'd burn his own CD for the ride he ran), playing on the midway after the fair closed for the night, and finding ways to humiliate the skids in every town. Darryl wouldn't be able to come along, of course, having to repeat all his high school classes for the rest of his life. Steffi, on the other hand, would. Sam then surprised himself by wondering if it might not be better to simply have a romance in every town, to be a devil-may-care ladies' man. He debated the possibilities while squeezing olive oil out of the neck of his T-shirt. Meanwhile, Steffi suggested milk-bottle bowling. Sam wiped his hands on his pants and reached for his money.

Sam was clutching a foot-long green plush snake, the everyone-wins-a-prize prize, when Darryl tapped him on the shoulder a while later. Sam had been so intent on winning a big prize and giving it to Steffi that he hadn't noticed Darryl's absence.

"I told you those games were a rip-off," Darryl said. "I explained the whole thing."

"I guess I didn't hear," Sam said. This year, he added silently. He didn't feel like acknowledging that Darryl had been right. The only one of the group to win anything good had been Delft, the new girl. Before moving to town she'd lived on a dairy farm. Sam had a feeling that somehow this gave her an edge at knocking over milk bottles. He didn't have a chance to explore this because Darryl was tugging him away from the group.

"Guess what you can do on the Gravitwirl."

"What?"

"Know what centrifunegual force is?"

"Centrifugal?"

"Whatever. You know, like when . . ." Darryl began to digress. It was hard to hear him. Sam knew from experience that the Gravitwirl was a ride. It spun you around so fast that you stuck to a wall. Then the floor dropped away.

"Darryl," he interrupted, "what can you do on the Gravitwirl?"

Darryl's eyes narrowed. "When it really gets spinning you can't move at all, right? Nothing. Not even your hand."

"So?"

"So it depends where your hand is." Darryl, it transpired, had spent the ride locked hand in hand with a girl in their French class. They could imagine other possibilities.

"Let's go on the Gravitwirl," Sam called. He got in line right behind Steffi.

They found places for themselves against the circular wall, next to some younger kids. Sam recognized Darryl's brother Ryan and his buddy Nick. Ryan had had a featured role in *The Music Man,* the latest production of the Hope Springs Players, and tomorrow he and Nick were in the talent show doing a comedy act. Sam got between Ryan and Steffi, casually bracing his hand on the wall a microscopic distance from Steffi's hemp bracelet. As the last riders climbed aboard, he heard Ryan ask something.

"Pardon?"

"How come you're wearing a helmet?"

"It's for the demolition derby," Sam said, by way of not really explaining. The boys seemed to accept this. Or maybe they were just distracted: they were looking hard at a moon-faced kid farther along the wall.

"What's up?" Sam asked, as the ride attendant shut the door. Suddenly he was too nervous to say anything to Steffi.

"That guy there, Travis," Ryan nodded at the moon-faced kid, "bet everybody he could ride ten times without puking. Last year he didn't make it."

"What? How many times has he been on so far?"

"Seven," Ryan called, and the ride began its first slow spin.

Seven? *Seven?* Sam looked at the kid as the ride accelerated, pushing everyone to the wall. He felt a twinge in his own stomach. The kid, Sam thought, definitely did not look happy. Maybe he should warn Steffi.

The colored lights were on now and the floor was dropping away. Kids were screaming in satisfaction. Sam felt pinned by a giant hand. Speaking of which. Warning Steffi would be the perfect reason for taking her hand. After he'd gotten her attention, he simply wouldn't be able to let go. He stretched out his fingers to tap Steffi's wrist. Would they touch palms or interlock fingers?

The wrist didn't seem to be there. Sam glanced again at the kid. He looked as if he was hearing shocking news about a pet kitten. *Uh-oh.* Sam fought to turn his head. It was a struggle, but Steffi was worth it.

The first thing he saw was that her near hand had migrated up by her ear. The second thing he saw, across the Himalayan peaks of her chest, was her other hand. It was clamped on the paw of a grade eleven skid famous for breaking a concrete block with his head. Currently he was upside down. Staggered by betrayal and incipient nausea, Sam wished the skid a landing on his concrete-proof skull. He tore his gaze away in time to see something coming straight at him.

"GAAH!" He flinched, which turned his head just enough to let whatever it was smack wetly into the side of the helmet. Beside him, Steffi shrieked. Something spattered his chest, then the air was rent with cries of outrage.

The Gravitwirl slowed. Lights and the floor came up to greet them, along with an appalling smell. The giant hand released its grip. The skid clunked down on his head. Down the wall, the moon-faced kid, swaying slightly, was wiping his mouth with the back of his hand. He looked relieved. Around him, horrified riders were flicking at clothes and dabbing their faces. A stampede for the exit had begun. Sam looked down at his own jersey. Splatters arced across his chest like bullet holes. He recognized popcorn chunks and a shred of onion ring before looking away. From beside him, over-riding the muffled din, was coming the sound of Steffi screaming.

He looked. Her face and streaked hair were liberally coated with something that might once have been corn dog. The stench was overpowering. Sam reached up to the helmet, then changed his mind. Gingerly, he shook his head instead. Foam scrunched. A pink glob of cotton candy landed wetly at his feet. Steffi screamed again and fled, tromping on the skid's paw as she went. It was a loud scream, even to Sam. He stepped carefully over the cotton candy and made his way to the exit. For the first time all day, it occurred to him that being stuck in a crash helmet might not be all bad.

Chapter

He woke up Saturday morning with a stiff neck and an oily pillow. The helmet was still on. It didn't hurt, really, except when the caliper headpiece on the earphones got pushed a certain way. The rest of the time there was just a modest pressure.

Sam lay in bed for a while reviewing the events of the night before. Steffi had eventually gone off with the concrete blockhead and some of his friends, leaving Sam with a pleasing feeling he identified as romantic regret. Actually, it felt more like relief. Either way, it was way better than *Lost*. Steffi was out of his system.

Now, apart from the helmet, the problem was that there was no point to helping at the derby. Darryl, the traitor, had been making plans with everybody else about all the things they'd do while Sam was stuck standing around on his own. Sam was worried that not only was he going to miss out on that stuff, he wouldn't be able to find anybody afterward, either. Then he'd have to listen to Darryl describe everything as they walked to school on Monday. But, since he'd asked Smitty to let him help, and since he needed Smitty to get the stupid helmet off, bailing out did not seem to be an option.

Neither did lying in bed any longer. Sam's neck was too sore and the pillowcase too slick. Besides, he was nervous about the talent show. (Although, maybe if they won he could get excused from the derby because everyone would insist he come to a big celebration. It was worth considering; a lot could happen in a day.)

Getting to the day was a chore in itself. The helmet made it tough changing jerseys and T-shirts. Sam had been particularly anxious to remove last night's. He'd even made sure to put it into the dirty clothes hamper. Shampooing, of course, was impossible. His head was feeling pretty swampy by now, but all he could do was bend in the shower, listening to the drumming effect the water made on his headgear.

"Maybe I'll see Smitty this morning," Mrs. Foster called as she bustled out the door. She had to open the Bulging Bin before heading off to another busy day helping to run the fair. "If not, you'll see him tonight at the derby. Hang in there." She stuck her head back through the doorway. "And goo-uck alley allen joe!"

"Huh?"

"GOOD LUCK AT THE TALENT SHOW!"

Which reminded Sam of the hearing problem. Since he was ADHD's drummer, it helped to hear the other instruments. "You have to play extra loud," he reminded Larry and Darryl as they prepared for a final run-through of the band's original tune, "Dragonsbreath." They were in the Fosters' garage. Out in the drive, Mr. Foster was stacking his trumpet and euphonium cases with some music stands. The Hope Springs Society Stompers were entertaining on the outdoor stage that afternoon and his band mate, Mr. Gernsbach, was going to give him, the boys, and the equipment a ride over in his truck. Darryl's dad would pick ADHD up after the talent show.

"But the mikes are as loud as they'll go," Larry complained. "If we play any louder we'll drown out the vocals." There was a pause as each of them silently considered whether this might not be a good thing.

"Let's try it again," said Darryl finally. "Last time."

Sam counted them off, tapping his drumstick against the side of the helmet, a nifty trick he'd thought of in the shower. They got all the way through, ending only a couple of beats apart. Robin looked in as the last power chord faded.

"Hey, 'Farts of Fire,' " she called. "I remember that one."

Being in the talent show got you free admission to the fair. Mr. Gernsbach drove them in to an orange Quonset hut that Hope Springers called the Pumpkin Palace. Over on the baseball diamond the strongman competition was getting underway, right beside the draft-horse judging. At the foot of the hill behind the Palace, a tractor and a forklift were shunting barriers into place for the demolition derby. Beyond the cattle and the petting zoo, the midway rides were going strong.

The boys toted drums, amplifiers, and guitars inside, past the prizewinning vegetables and preserves, the arts and crafts show, and the cake bakeoff. In the middle of the Palace a small stage had been erected, with two microphones on stands. An optimistic number of chairs had been put out for an audience, with a table for the judges.

Some of the other performers were already there. Mrs. Stewart, who always ran the talent show, told them when they'd be on and let Sam set up his drums ahead of time. Robin appeared, snapping pictures with a digital camera. It had turned out she actually was helping cover the fair for the *Eternal*.

"Put us on the front page," suggested Larry.

"Yeah, make us famous," Darryl chimed in. "On second thought, make me famous." He stepped in front of Sam and Larry, spread his arms, and made a goggle-eyed face. At the moment, this was fine with Sam. Being immortalized in a crash helmet was something he didn't need. Not that Darryl's goofing around mattered: Sam had forgotten that his band mates came up no higher than his chin. Without a stepladder Darryl wouldn't be blocking Sam out of anything. Before Sam could bend his knees to hide, Robin had taken the shot. She showed them the readout on the screen. Sam looked like an ostrich. Darryl's ears flapped in a nonexistent breeze. Larry's fly was at half-mast. "Perfect," Robin said and strode away before they could protest.

The three judges arrived, then an audience. Well, almost an audience: at certain moments the judges outnumbered it. Sam didn't mind. He was so nervous that he could barely feel the drumsticks in his hand. This was, after all, ADHD's first public performance. Even though the band was sandwiched between a ten-year-old juggler and old Mr. Tompkins, who did impressions of fruit, it felt like a big deal. Everybody had to start somewhere, as Mr. Foster liked to say.

Fidgeting backstage, Sam looked at the others. Larry and Darryl had that pale, haunted look your classmates got right before an exam they'd forgotten to study for. Sam remembered the times they'd all skipped practicing. Out front, the audience laughed at something that Sam couldn't hear through the helmet. It sounded as if it had grown bigger. Darryl scowled and looked at the floor. The audience laughed again. Darryl shifted the burden of the electric guitar strapped over his shoulder. Its body was shaped—ludicrously, in Sam's opinion—like a stylized lightning bolt. At the moment it could have been blasting out of Darryl's eyeballs.

"Who's out there?" Sam asked.

Darryl's brow cleared instantly. "Ryan and Nick," he said, in a possessive tone that implied he'd already signed his brother to an exclusive management contract. "Have you seen their act? They are sooooo funny. Melissa helped them rehearse." Melissa was Darryl's older sister. She too had been a star with the Hope Springs Players, one year appearing as Dorothy in *The Wizard of Oz*. Now, like Robin, she was away at university. She had a scholarship and she'd joined the volleyball team, Darryl reported, the day before he'd quit cross-country. Darryl was still describing the act they were not seeing when a robust burst of applause ushered the two comics offstage. They appeared, grinning and red-faced, as Mrs. Stewart bustled up. "Okay, ADHD, you're next."

"But what about the juggler?" Larry protested.

"He dropped his eggs. We'll put him on later. Come on, guys, let's go."

They stumbled out. Sam tried to settle himself behind his drum kit as the others plugged in. He looked everywhere but at the audience. Everything seemed a shade too near or too far away for comfort. Mrs. Stewart introduced them. His band mates turned deer-in-the-headlights gazes on him. Sam took a breath and began tapping his helmet, too fast, he realized. Too late.

They raced through "Dragonsbreath" in record time. Larry forgot the words, Sam forgot his fills, and Darryl dropped all the picks he'd planned to toss out to the nonexistent cheering audience. Not that it mattered: the acoustics in the Pumpkin Palace were so bad that, even to Sam's congested ears, ADHD sounded like a nauseated rototiller. They shuffled off to tepid applause from the judges, Larry's parents, and Ryan.

Nobody said anything until they were carrying the equipment out to Darryl's dad's van.

"Wait till I get my five-string bass," Larry said.

"I don't think my effects pedal is responding on all its frequencies," Darryl panted. He'd had to hurry to catch up, having stayed behind to round up his dropped picks. They weren't cheap, picks.

Sam merely nodded glumly. Another drop of oil oozed down his neck. His friends' faces told him what they were really thinking. What they were thinking was what he was thinking. ADHD bit, big-time.

Mr. Sweeney helped arrange things in the van. By the time they got back inside the Pumpkin Palace to collect another load, Mr. Tompkins had finished his fruit impressions and Mrs. Stewart was introducing someone whose name Sam did not catch. He was stepping around an open oven door as they passed through the cake bakeoff when Darryl said, "What zits!" and Larry said, "Hubba hubba." Sam looked up, and Madison Dakota hit him straight between the ears.

Chapter

He hustled backstage. In the blink of an eye, *Lost* had supplied an entire romantic saga, with a Frog Prince theme. Touched by his plea for help, Madison Dakota would hit that note again, popping off the helmet, whereupon she'd see the true Sam and ask about the drumsticks in his hand. He'd confess to musical ability, mention his band. They'd agree to meet at the derby, they'd feel the tug of deeper feelings . . . All this depended, of course, on her not having heard how bad ADHD had truly been.

He ducked around the 4-H bulletin board. She was gone.

"Where's that singer that was just on?" he asked Nick. A picture of a cornstalk seemed to be sprouting from his head. Nick shrugged. "She left."

Mr. Tompkins, still kibitzing, was no help either. "Watch this: a banana," he said when Sam asked him about the girl. Mr. Tompkins's hearing was nothing to write home about. He pushed his pomaded hair into a point and curved his body forward in a gentle arc. In his yellow leisure suit, he did look something like a banana.

Sam hurried on. She hadn't come out front, so that meant she must have gone out the far door, past the model train exhibit. He ran. A wide assortment of people were strolling by, none of them babes in cowboy hats. There was a knock on his helmet. He turned to see Smitty, resplendent in his usual garb of T-shirt and green work pants. Sam described who he was looking for.

"Nope, didn't see her," Smitty said. "What's with the crash helmet?"

"Somebody stuck it on my head. Can you help me get it off?" A chance to get rid of the helmet was too good to pass up.

Smitty resettled his own cap, inscribed BALD ON TOP, and peered at the problem from several angles. Then he gripped the helmet between his massive hands and tugged.

"Yow!" Sam writhed.

Smitty's hands slipped off. He wiped them on his work pants. "Geez, Sam. Whattya got in there?"

Sam explained about the olive oil and the earphones. Smitty shook his head and blew a gum bubble. "I'm gonna need tools. I could cut it off. Anyway, I don't have time right now. Maybe after the derby."

"Do you still need me there? For the whole thing?"

"Yeah, sure." Smitty was not taking the hint that it was fine if Sam were excused. "In fact, a helmet may not be a bad idea. Be there at six."

Sam got back to the talent contest as the judges announced Madison Dakota the winner. She'd had to leave, they said, but her ten-dollar prize would be mailed to her.

"What was with you?" Larry asked. "Where'd you have to go?"

"I thought I forgot something. Then I saw Smitty."

"Oh yeah," Larry remembered something. "Doug said to tell you Norm says he wants his helmet back tonight or else."

The boys took the last of their equipment to the van, Sam glumly watching for a cowboy hat. Larry suggested food. Darryl said no. He was saving his money for later. A big evening was clearly in the offing.

"Why don't you guys meet me after the derby?" Sam suggested.

"Well, I don't know exactly what we're going to be doing," Darryl looked off in every direction but Sam's. "I'm not even sure if we'll still be here."

"Oh." Before he even knew it, Sam was walking away.

"Hey, where ya going?" called Darryl. He sounded worried that Sam might this instant be going to a party without him.

"I've got stuff to do."

He didn't have stuff to do, any more than he had a party to go to. Right now it was just all too much. He was stuck in some ape-man's helmet, ADHD had sucked out loud, Darryl was trying to shut him out, and a dream girl had vanished. He'd hit rock-bottom. Sam climbed the steps to the Fair Board trailer, where his mom was busy signing checks.

"How was the talent show?" was the first thing she asked.

"It was okay," Sam lied. "I'll tell you later." Like, in fifty years. He changed the subject. "I have to be here to help Smitty at six. He thinks he can get the helmet off."

"Thank heavens for that," said Mrs. Foster. "Meet me at four and I'll give you a ride home."

"I think I'll just walk now. I've had enough fair for a while."

At home, he sat in the backyard and listened to nothing. This was unfortunate, because it kept his mind running on a shadowy circuit crowded with thoughts about friendless evenings, and Norm saying "or else."

What did "or else" mean? He didn't want to think about it.

He tried to think about Madison Dakota instead. Who was she? Sam had never heard the name before, never seen her around school. Maybe she went to Saint Tiffany's in Cobourg. Maybe she was new and she'd show up at Hope Springs High on Monday. Or maybe—he sat up straight at this—she'd be at the demolition derby tonight. Which changed the whole helmet picture. Granted he'd look like a dork going up to her in the helmet, but having her sing it off was such a romantic introduction it was hard to let it go. He was almost glad he was stuck like this. After all, if you went up to a girl with a flame-decalled crash helmet stuck on your head, there was no place to go but up.

Or was there? What if he didn't find Madison Dakota? Norm would want the helmet before he drove. Smitty had said he could cut the helmet off. Sam's imagination offered up a vision of a giant buzz-saw blade descending toward his brain. He squirmed back down in his lawn chair. He had a feeling Norm wouldn't be too pleased with this solution, either. And assuming he survived, it would probably mean he'd have to buy Norm a new helmet—even though the whole thing had not been his fault. What did crash helmets cost, anyway?

"Hunnerd and twenny-five bucks," Norm glared at him over the hood of the Junk Yard Dawg that night. "Minimum." They were standing down in the staging area for demolition derby cars. Behind them, contestants in an early heat were bashing away at each other. Nonetheless, Norm's voice was more than loud enough to hear.

"Don't worry," Sam pleaded, trying not to twitch. An itch had begun to insinuate itself above his right ear. He also felt like a target in his Day-Glo vest. "I'm working on it." *Oh God*, he prayed, *let Madison Dakota be here.*

"Yeah, and meantime I gotta wear this effin' thing. Looks stupid." Norm brandished a plain white helmet that had all the flair of a fat man on a moped.

"It's not my fault. Somebody did it to me. I don't look any better."

"Hey," Norm warned. "Don't say nothing bad about my helmet. That is an effin' great helmet. And don't scratch at it like that!"

Sam jerked his hand away. He hadn't even realized he'd been trying to get at the itch.

"You'll peel the decals off," Norm groused. "You wreck it, you pay for it."

Sam shuffled back to the safety barriers in time to watch the losing cars from the first round being hauled out of the ring. A pall of smoke and dust floated beneath the overhead lights. The hill behind the Pumpkin Palace was packed. The volunteer fire department and the ambulance crew stood nearby. The PA blared the names of the next contestants. The itch was getting worse. Sam pushed the helmet even farther down on his head. The rubbing helped a little. *God,* he thought again, *please send Madison Dakota. If you do, I'll help Smitty for free, forever.*

He turned to the lurid glow of the midway to see if there'd be an answer. The Ferris wheel turned in stately condescension. The Zipper and the Magic Carpet flung themselves into the night sky, leaving a contrail of screams behind. These were not answers. He swung back to the hillside, eyes straining for a glimpse of gingham shirt or cascading curls. There were too many people; he couldn't even spot the cluster of friends he'd seen earlier. He was doomed. Abandoned and doomed. And after Smitty finished sawing, he'd be abandoned and doomed and owe Norm one hundred and twenty-five dollars. Plus he had homework, and what if he was bald or something when the helmet came off? And he was ITCHING. *Eff,* he thought, Norm-style. *Eff, eff, eff, eff, eff.*

Sam was so busy swearing that at first he didn't recognize either of the people strolling toward him. Maybe it was also because they seemed so out of place. Nonetheless, one was Mrs. Goodenough. The man with her was not J. Earl. He was about Sam's height, with a mane of silvery hair and a close-cropped beard of the same color. Both he and Mrs. Goodenough looked far too dressy for the fair, she in a long, dark skirt with a flamboyant sweater, he in black trousers and a collarless shirt, with a linen jacket draped cape-style over his shoulders. Mrs. Goodenough was smoking a cigarette.

"Sam," she announced, remembering to speak louder because of the helmet. "Just the person we need. Sam, this is Sidney Glebe, an old friend of mine. Sid, Sam Foster."

Glebe extended a pale hand with very long fingers. Sam shook it tentatively.

"Sid here is curious about how a demolition derby works. I was hoping you could explain it to him."

"Oh. Sure." Sam nodded. The next contestants came roaring into the ring, the Junk Yard Dawg among them. Mrs. Goodenough winced at the noise; Glebe appeared not to notice. He pulled a black object about the size of Mr. Foster's electric shaver from his pocket and pressed a button. "The cars all bash each other and the last one running wins," Sam said. "Then the winner goes to the final and they bash each other there."

The announcer led the crowd into the countdown to the starting flag. The drivers revved their engines.

"And there's a whole stragety to it," Sam shouted above the roar, mispronouncing the word the way he always did. He could see how Darryl might enjoy this. Besides, it took his mind off his troubles. "What you try to do is—"

"CAN WE GET AWAY FROM THE NOISE A LITTLE?" Mrs. Goodenough shouted. Behind them, metal crunched. The crowd aahhed.

As they left the barrier, a volunteer firefighter approached. He had the build of a fire hydrant, which seemed appropriate. It turned out to be Mr. Gernsbach, who had given the band a drive that morning.

"'Scuse me, folks," he said loudly. "Sam, listen, man. Can you hear me okay?" Sam nodded. "Your dad was telling me about this helmet scene. I told the guys. We've got our Jaws of Life rig over there. We can pry it off."

Sam felt a flicker of hope. "Would it wreck the helmet?"

"Depends."

"What's the problem?" Glebe's eyebrows climbed his forehead. The silver mane didn't start until you got well up there.

"The helmet is stuck on his head," Mrs. Goodenough explained more quietly from behind, or, as Sam heard it, "Elma uckon hihea."

Glebe tilted his own head. His nostrils flared as he considered the problem. "There's an easier way," he said from far off, "that won't damage anything. Come over to my car."

O. Sidney Glebe led the way to the parking lot in a loose-limbed slouch that managed to be casual and commanding at the same time. The adults made indistinct noises that Sam took to be introductions. He was too stunned by the apparent change in his fortunes to pay much attention. Mr. Gernsbach and Glebe continued to talk. Mrs. Goodenough dropped back beside Sam.

"Don't worry," she said to Sam, "Siddy's a whiz at this kind of thing. You never know what he'll come up with next."

"Is he the composer?" Sam asked. It was all he could think of to say. Behind them, the noise of the derby stopped. Ahead of them, he saw Glebe take what could have been plugs from his ears.

Mrs. Goodenough nodded and flicked her cigarette butt away. "And more. Luckily for you, a Renaissance man, Sam. Unlike some others I could mention."

Sam didn't fully take this in. Too much was happening. They had arrived at Glebe's car, where the Renaissance man was opening his trunk. At the same moment, the itch intensified. And then Sam heard an announcement back at the derby:

" . . . GIVE US A TUNE DURING THE DELAY . . . THIS YEAR'S TALENT CONTEST WINNER . . . ON . . . AKOTA."

"What?" Sam spun around.

"Whoah, now," Mr. Gernsbach caught Sam's shoulder. "Let's do this, man."

"But—"

"It's very simple," Glebe was saying to the world in general. He opened a black briefcase. Inside, nestled in a notched foam lining, lay three rows of gleaming . . . somethings. For a panicky instant, Sam thought they might be surgical instruments.

"Tuning forks," said Glebe, holding one up. It was an elongated chromium U, on a stem that ended in a shiny ball about the size of a pea. "We'll use sound waves to solve your problem."

"Good vibrations, man," nodded Mr. Gernsbach. His fire helmet was off. You could see where he'd pinned up his silver ponytail.

"But—" Sam didn't know what they were talking about. Meanwhile, country karaoke was wafting from the fairground. *She was singing.* He had to get back there. "But," he said again. "But—"

"It's just a matter of selecting the right pitch and frequency," Glebe said, ignoring Sam's protests. He surveyed the forks. His eyes narrowed in concentration. Sam rocked from foot to foot. The music spun on.

"We'll try these." Glebe at last took a tuning fork in each hand. He held the stems delicately, between thumbs and lengthy forefingers. "The instant you feel things loosen, push. Carl," he said to Mr. Gernsbach, "stand by."

Sam was all but bouncing with frustration. At the fair, the tune was building. He *had* to get back there. Glebe rapped the tuning forks smartly on either side of the helmet, then touched the rounded ends to points over Sam's ears. An odd, humming discord filled Sam's brain, blotting out everything else. It was the sonic equivalent of the yellow-green glow he got when he rubbed his eyes. Vibrations tingled through the helmet. The itch ran wild across his scalp. Then the pressure magically eased, the way it had when Madison Dakota hit her note. The helmet wobbled. Sam scrunched his eyes shut, shot his hands up, and pushed.

At his first touch everything stopped. The vise grabbed at his scalp again, only now it was a little higher up—and slipping. Mr. Gernsbach was helping, prying the helmet sides as wide as they'd go. The pressure crept upward as the front of the helmet began a slow-motion topple toward his nose, accompanied by the drawn-out scrunching of foam in his ears. He pushed harder. The itch went right off the scale, causing him to do a writhing, hunched-over dance step at the same time.

"C'mon, baby," Mr. Gernsbach grunted through the static. "It's almost there."

And then it was. With a last desperate grab at his temples, Norm's flaming pride and joy popped off. Mr. Gernsbach lifted it clear. Night air rushed at Sam's head even faster than his own desperately scratching fingers. Digging through his hair was like fondling a Caesar salad.

"Ahhhhhhhhhhh," he drew out a sigh of relief as the itching stopped. He straightened, wiped his hands on his pants, then pulled the CD phones from his ears, then wiped his hands again.

The adults stood looking at him. "Wow," Sam panted. "Uh, thank you."

"Not a problem." Glebe waved the tuning forks rather like conductors' batons. Sam could hear him far more clearly, not to mention the music from the fairground. The music from the fairground! He grabbed the helmet.

"I gotta get back," he blurted. "Like, uh, before they . . . *Thanks.*"

He was already running. It was rude, but this was an emergency. Behind him, he heard Mr. Gernsbach saying, "Yeah man, buzzard ugly. That was . . ." Then all he heard was olive oil chugging in his ears and Madison Dakota's over-amplified voice belting the final drawn-out notes of whatever she'd been karaokeing to. He sprinted across the ball diamond, Day-Glo vest flapping, helmet in hand, as the last notes of music dissolved into desultory applause and whistles, followed by the announcer: "ALL RIGHT, ALL RIGHT, WE'RE READY TO ROLL. LET'S ROCK 'EM AND SOCK 'EM THERE, BOYS!"

Engines roared, and the crowd cheered.

"Noooooo!" Sam redoubled his effort across right field. It was no use. By the time he got back to the barriers, Madison Dakota was gone. Norm was slumped disconsolately behind the wheel of the motionless Dawg, which was accordioned at both ends like something from a cartoon. Sam held up the helmet. Norm glared and flipped him the bird. Sam sagged and turned away.

"Perfect," said a familiar voice.

He looked up. Robin had just taken his picture again. "I can see the caption," she said. *"Demo Derby A Hair-Raising Experience."*

The shot came up on the camera's screen. Olive oil and fingers had given Sam a unique hairstyle. Combined with the Day-Glo vest it gave him the appearance of an underfed scarecrow.

"Don't print it," Sam pleaded. He'd had enough today.

"I don't know, Sam." Robin smiled her most evil big-sister grin. "This one might cost you."

Chapter

"We bit at the talent contest," Sam confessed. He pulled his math text from his locker. All around was the clanking of metal doors and the hubbub of pre-class conversation, mixed with the occasional burp from Steve.

"That's too bad," Amanda said. She and Delft were waiting for him. Darryl, who had filled the walk to school with a breathless description of the incredible things he'd done Saturday night, did not have the same math class, thankfully. His marks being what they were, Darryl was taking applied-level subjects instead of academic, except for his music option.

"Aw, it wouldn't have mattered anyway," Sam continued his confession. Neither girl had, in fact, asked about the contest, but this was all part of the plan. Operation Babe Find had begun. He clicked his combination lock shut and gave the dial a spin. "There was this girl singer who blew everybody right out of the water."

"Oh."

Neither Amanda nor Delft seemed interested in girl singers. Delft was already asking, "Did anybody get the last two questions?" Sam persevered with what he felt was admirable subtlety.

"Yeah, her name was Madison something."

"Wisconsin," suggested Amanda. "Were those the questions about volume?"

"No," Sam said. "It was like Dacron or Kodak or something."

"One was the volume of a pyramid," Delft said. They began the walk to class, joining a flood tide of skids and jocks and nerds and preps, Goths, punks, water-walkers, and hippies.

"What, number fourteen? That was, uh, three thousand four hundred cubic—"

"The weird thing is," Sam shrugged, "I thought I knew all the music people around here." This was stretching things. The inaugural rehearsal of the school band had been the biggest gathering of more or less musicians he'd ever seen. Still, the girls seemed to accept his claim.

"I got that one," Amanda said. "But not the area of a pentagon." They started down the stairs.

"So, like, neither of you know her, eh?" Sam sniffed to show how idle his curiosity was. "Long dark hair, country music—"

"*Country* music?" Amanda squinched her nose. "She probably goes to St. Tiffany's."

"Yeah," Delft agreed. "I know a girl who goes there named Brooklyn."

"Oh yeah? Could you—"

"Did you get five hundred and seventy-two square yards?"

"Yeah. Hey Sam, there's your dad."

Operation Babe Find went on hold. Sam instantly dropped into Survival Slouch. Sure enough, his father was at the bottom of the stairs, talking to two hippie-looking students. For years, Mr. Foster had taught kindergarten at O. P. Doberman, Sam's old school. There, it had been okay having your dad down the hall. Almost everyone liked kindergarten, and a nearby parent had been handy for rides and whatnot. Then Mr. Foster had declared he needed a new challenge, and here he was, the drama teacher. "We'll go to high school together," he'd said to Sam. "Just kidding," he'd said into the silence that followed.

Sam had not laughed. High school was not a place for your dad to be, knowing every single thing you did. Not that Sam did much of anything. It was the principle of the thing. Robin had cruised through without anyone peering over her shoulder, even when she'd shaved half her head, dyed the other half orange, and gotten her nose pierced. It wasn't fair. God, it was bad enough having teachers remember Robin, bad enough having skids ask, "Hey string-bean, how's the weather up there?" What would happen when everyone found out his dad was the guy who made you pretend to be saplings bending in the wind?

As they reached the foot of the stairs, Sam, still Slouching, flicked a cautious glance Dad-ward. Mr. Foster arched an eyebrow in return and went on talking. Sam zipped through the stairwell doors. It wasn't until he was well down the hall that he unwound a little. Maybe he'd overreacted. At least his dad didn't look too dorky: no Mr. Gernsbach-style ponytail or cool-guy clothes like their history teacher wore. That guy was at least thirty and still, sadly, trying to look young.

By lunchtime, it occurred to him that his music teacher might actually know musicians the way Sam had claimed to. Furthermore, it would be less risky asking Mr. Carnoostie about a girl than it would be asking girls about a girl. After enduring Darryl's lecture about Jimi Hendrix for most of a cheese sandwich, Sam headed for music early, keeping a sharp lookout for his dad, whose drama room was next door.

Mr. Carnoostie was sorting handouts at his lectern. He was a large and ebullient man whose red cheeks gave the impression that he had been inflated.

"Can't say that I've heard of her, Sam. Does she sing in a choir or anything? I know most of those kids." Mr. Carnoostie often helped with local musical events.

"I don't know. She's got all this dark hair, and she sings country music."

"Well, that's not really my thing, but I'll keep my ears open." Mr. Carnoostie grinned. "Do you know who O. Sidney Glebe is, Sam?"

"Yeah. He's this composer." Sam was about to add that he'd met him, when he remembered where and shut his mouth.

"Right. Good for you. In fact, a very famous one." Mr. Carnoostie vigorously squared his stack of papers. "He's doing a work about Hope Springs, and I've persuaded him to come and give a workshop for you guys here at the school. Isn't that great?"

"Wow," Sam agreed insincerely. He slunk to his chair. Maybe Glebe wouldn't recognize him without a helmet and olive oil. It had been dark, after all. He hadn't had too much teasing about the helmet since it came off, but he was still worried that one of Robin's pictures of him might be in today's *Eternal*. When he finally did meet Madison Dakota, he didn't want her to think of *that*. Maybe they could laugh over it later—like, twenty years from now—but not yet. For solace, he started work on an elaborate MADISON DAKOTA doodle on the inner flap of his music folder.

Fortunately, as he found out after school, none of the incriminating photos had made the paper. Unfortunately, there was nothing about Madison Dakota, either. The talent show pictures were of the Gunderson twins doing their teacup dance and Darryl's brother getting a pie in the face at the end of his comedy act. It didn't matter. Sam could still picture that waterfall of dark curls, that gingham-knotted midriff, hear the catch and wail in that voice. He wondered what she'd sound like singing "Farts of . . ."— or rather, "Dragonsbreath."

But wait—that was it! Sam dropped the newspaper on the hall table and savored his inspiration. She wouldn't sing "Farts of Fire," because he'd invite Madison to sing in a new band! And, unfortunately, he'd forget to invite Darryl to join. In fact, he wouldn't invite anyone to join until just the two of them had gotten together on their own a few times to run over some tunes.

This would also remove the possibility of her remembering anyone from the talent show (and how bad they were), or of anyone else, like Darryl, horning in before she could fall in love with Sam. Sam was pretty sure that he'd go unrecognized, what with the fiery crash helmet and all. A bigger problem would be how he and

Madison would run over tunes, seeing as how he didn't play anything but drums. He wondered how long it would take to learn guitar. Robin had a guitar she'd abandoned after three lessons; his dad had offered to show him some chords. And wouldn't that show Darryl, when he blew him away on his own instrument? All right, then. As Sam went to hunt up the guitar, he was beginning to feel this was all meant to be. All he really had to do was find her.

Just how he was going to do *that* was still unclear. Looking at the *Eternal,* he wondered about putting in an ad for a girl singer, but after a weekend at the fall fair he didn't have the money to do it. But heck, in a town the size of Hope Springs, you couldn't remain mysterious very long. If Madison Dakota didn't go to Hope Springs High, Sam had to put himself in some other places. Thus it was that he accepted his mother's offer of a few hours' work at the store the following Saturday. As Mrs. Foster often dryly put it, sooner or later everyone ended up in the Bin.

Sam blearily arrived for the eleven-to-two shift, covering lunches. He'd been up late the night before, video gaming with Darryl and Steve, so his defenses were down as he passed the gaggle of skids already huddled at Lint Lane. There were three boys and two girls, all of whom Sam recognized as grade elevens and all No-Hopers. This meant that they had gone to the rural North Hope School before the High.

"Streeeetch," said one, perched on the mailbox.

"Grade ni-ine," intoned another, the *nine* dipping into a mock-bass. Too late, Sam went into Survival Slouch mode and ducked into the store.

Over his protests, his mom kitted him out in a white apron that would have been long if Sam had been shorter. She left him with a list of chores to begin in the first hour, when he'd be alone, as well as strict instructions not to change the classical music station on the radio. Unlike Sam, Bulging Bin patrons were not always fans of Razor 101.3, the *Cutting Edgedgedgedge* of Rock Radio.

Mrs. Foster headed out, but Madison Dakota did not come in. Instead Darryl did, apparently just to let Sam know that he'd be missing a trip to the mall in Oshawa by working. Sam cooled his irritation by stocking the freezer at the back of the store. The door chimed. He looked up hopefully. Was it . . . ? A couple of the skids galumphed in and began studying herbal remedies for arthritis. Sam stared. There was rustling beyond them. He heard the slamming of bin lids. When he moved to see what was going on, the arthritic pair moved, blocking his view.

Sam turned uneasily back to the freezer. What should he do? He knew what his mom, all five foot four of her, would do: march up to them and, in her cheery ex-gym teacher's voice, ask what they were looking for, all the while herding them gently back to the door. Something told Sam that approach would not work for him. He closed the freezer and started down the other aisle, toward the front counter. The skids moved deeper into the store. The door chimed again, admitting old Mrs. Steener, in for her weekly supply of oat bran, and Mr. Tompkins, who had a passion for candied papaya spears. As the two customers reached the counter, the skids smirked their way out, huddled like fugitives from a chain gang. The last paused to emit a long, soggy lip fart. On the sidewalk, the others howled.

This last touch was lost on Sam's hard-of-hearing customers.

"Been working on a bunch of grapes," Mr. Tompkins, the fruit imitator, obliviously informed them. He bulged his eyes, puffed his cheeks and elevated his chin into a tight little ball, while holding circled fingers to his temples. It was quite effective, particularly as his face reddened with the effort.

Mrs. Steener, just as deaf, observed, "If you're that constipated, Bernie, get some oat bran."

Sam simply nodded politely as he rang in the sales. His back was to the front window. He could hear, from the sidewalk, the muffled sounds of skid derision. Someone hooted. Someone swore. Someone bumped the window. Sam felt even thinner than he was.

He didn't turn around. He didn't want to look in the candy bins, either. As his customers left, he looked instead for a long moment at the sticker his mom had placed below the cash on the business side of the counter: WHY CALL IT TOURIST SEASON IF YOU CAN'T SHOOT THEM? With Madison Dakota temporarily forgotten, he went back to the freezer, trying to come up with variations about skids.

He hadn't come up with anything by the time his mom returned. Sam told her about the invasion. Mrs. Foster nodded. "Don't worry, Sammy. It's not your fault."

Sam nodded in relief.

"You know," Mrs. Foster went on, "something has to be done about those kids. And you just might be able to help."

Sam stopped nodding.

Chapter 8

It took Sam two weeks and a ride on a white horse to grasp the full import of his mom's comment. By then, he had more or less forgotten it. He'd had assorted regular homework, a French quiz, a math test, an English assignment, a cross-country meet, two drum lessons, some basic guitar instruction from his dad, and some resultant sore fingers. Mr. Foster had clearly enjoyed bonking around with the guitar, an instrument from his youth that he'd left behind as he'd gotten more and more into old-time jazz. He even knew the chords to some Jimi Hendrix tunes. Sam practiced them when not doing everything else, including having an ADHD practice, enduring more runarounds from Darryl, and, more importantly, having a brilliant idea about Madison Dakota.

Back at the talent show, Mrs. Stewart had said they'd mail the winning check to her. Therefore Mrs. Stewart knew where she lived. Sam worked up the courage to call and ask for the address. He told Mrs. Stewart that ADHD was looking for a singer. She agreed that was a very good idea. Unfortunately, she said, she couldn't offer any help.

"Madison really wants her privacy, Sam. I promised her not to give out any information."

"Oh. Well, but, like . . . can you tell me even if she's from around here?" There was no point in being *Lost* over someone who'd jetted in from the coast.

Mrs. Stewart, who knew Sam, chuckled and gave in a little. "Yes, she's local. Why don't you watch the *Eternal,* see if she's performing anywhere else? I know she's done lots of things in the past."

"Really?"

"Really. Good luck."

He'd been combing the Coming Events column in the *Eternal* ever since, to no avail, and frankly, he was about ready to give up. Now, it was suppertime on a Friday. Mr. Foster was dishing up helpings of his specialty, Lentils Supreme. Sam was saying he wasn't very hungry and praying he'd have time to buy fries before the movie he was going to. Amanda and Steve had let him know Darryl was rounding up moviegoers, though he'd never mentioned it to Sam. What had happened to his best friend?

At the dinner table, Mrs. Foster was pouring herself a second glass of wine and summing up a meeting of the Downtown Business Association.

"Anyway," she sighed, "the nitty-gritty was how the kids who hang around Lint Lane are driving away business. Bert Hoogstratten is fit to be tied about it."

This was Delft's dad. The Hoogstrattens now ran the flower shop across from the Bulging Bin. Sam had some milk and pushed the beans around on his plate, trying to remember the chords his dad had showed him for "Hey Joe," a classic Hendrix song.

"There's nothing to do about it," Mr. Foster said, tucking into his first helping. "It's a Hope Springs tradition. The only place you could drive them away to is a mall, and if we had a mall we wouldn't have a downtown worth worrying about."

"Okay," Mrs. Foster said, "but what if we had a teen space downtown, something especially for them? You know, where they could skateboard or play their boom boxes or kick those little baggy things around."

"Hackysacks," Sam supplied, absently.

"Right. Their own space."

"To smoke and litter and swear in." Mr. Foster cheerfully spooned up more lentils.

"Better there than next to my store. God, I hate it when they start spitting—or blowing their noses."

"Blowing their noses?"

"The farmer blow," Sam filled in again, automatically, as he maneuvered a lentil behind his salad. Skids seldom carried anything as effete as tissues, so nasal blockage was handled by pinching one nostril with a finger and firing the other at the sidewalk.

"Maybe if it was their space they'd look after it," Mrs. Foster said, sipping her wine. "What do you think, Sam? Would kids go for that?"

Sam knew the answer: no. But how could you explain to grownups that the whole point of hanging around Lint Lane was that it bugged people? No one would want to go to a place where they were *supposed* to be. He brushed the hair out of his eyes and shrugged.

"Exactly," said his mom, as if he'd agreed wholeheartedly. "The DBA is divided about this, so we need to get some public support."

That "we" didn't sound right. Sam drained his milk. "I've got to go now. I don't want to be late."

"So I'm starting a petition," Mrs. Foster continued as he rose, "and I want you to see if you can round up some kids to help. If business, teens, church, and school present it to town council together, we'll have them cold."

"Gee, Mom, I don't think I can do that right now. I've got, like, tons of homework, and there's this project almost due and school band and drum lessons and . . ." Sam continued the list as he hightailed it down the hall, mentioning everything he could think of except Operation Babe Find. It didn't matter that the skids bugged him, too. There was no way he was going to help a bunch of grownups meddle in teen loitering. What kind of a suck-up did his mom want him to look like, anyway?

The movie, *Gutbuster,* was a frat-house comedy featuring a running gag about canine flatulence and way more zit-free skin than Sam's mom would probably have liked. Not that it mattered: no one was there for the movie, certainly not the couple three rows down who necked all the way through it. High school weekends were not places you wanted to be alone in; you went to the movies with your friends to, well, *be* there. That way you could join in the Monday morning replays of your group's wild exploits—or at least, the exploits you tried to make sound wild.

Sam was grateful to Amanda and Steve for making sure to include him, even though he knew the truth was that a group made up of Steve, Larry, Darryl, Amanda, Ashley, himself, and Delft Hoogstratten was about as wild as a free-range marshmallow. He couldn't help thinking that things would be different if he were with Madison Dakota.

Still, everyone did their best. Steve rattled off some burps. Larry and Amanda dueled with limp licorice twizzles. Ashley started a brief popcorn war to shut down Darryl's explanation of beer keg physics.

After the show they walked back through town. It was a chilly night and, except for the sidewalk in front of Jimmy's Pizza, the streets were relatively skidless. Sam was still distracted by the panorama of *Gutbuster* cleavage that had been on view. One of the actresses had stirred definite *Lost* feelings. Since she was no more unattainable than Madison Dakota, he was indulging in a brief fantasy in which they met backstage while his band was on a world tour. Now, as they reached the parking lot of the Hoo Lee Garden restaurant, he snapped out of it: genuine teen action was taking place: Larry was riding a horse.

Not a real horse. The entrance to the Hoo Lee parking lot was flanked by concrete statues of rearing horses, painted white. What these had to do with take-out Chinese food was anybody's guess, but sooner or later even the meekest teen in Hope Springs got the urge to climb aboard and pose idiotically for his or her friends. It was even more satisfying if Mr. Larose, who owned the place, saw you and blustered out to chase you away. Then you had the full experience. "Oh yeah?" you could say whenever the subject came up. "Did he see you? Oh man, when I did it he came bombing out of there like he had a firecracker up his butt. He was sooooo mad."

Clinging to the arching concrete neck, Larry yahooed into the October night.

"What a dough-head," Ashley said admiringly.

Larry awkwardly reached down from his perch to swat at her with the remaining licorice twizzle. "Giddyap!" Then, "Whoah!" as he almost slipped.

Amanda tugged Larry down and deftly scrambled up herself, managing to pose, standing, like a circus bareback rider, for an instant before losing her balance. That did it: the race for a Monday morning legend had begun. "Everybody on!" Darryl ordered.

Boosting and hauling was necessary. Sam, clambering, found himself amazingly close to various parts of various female bodies. He did everything but gulp as a general sense of *Lost* re-enveloped him. They were all *friends*. Still. The boys talked about the girls, sometimes. Who knew what the girls talked about? Sam and Amanda had been sort-of buddies after Sam abandoned his passion for Ms. Broom. Lately, Darryl had been mentioning Delft in breaks from his analysis of the Hendrix guitar style. Sam, of course, dreamed of a certain cowgirl, and the combination of girls and white horses brought her galloping back to mind. Hadn't Delft said she knew a girl named Baltimore who . . . ? The wild times made Sam bold. Why not ask her right now? Quietly, of course.

Delft was most of the way up a horse's neck. Maybe farm life had prepared her for horse statue climbing as well as milk-bottle bowling. Sam made a little jump and caught hold of the horse's flaring ears. It was easy for someone his height. Chinning himself to get close enough to ask a private question was harder, bodybuilding being still on his to-do list. Nonetheless, he managed to huff up as far as the horse's blank, white eye before croaking, "Hey, Delft?"

Delft looked down at him. As she did, she lost her grip and spilled forward onto the horse's head, bringing her nose to nose with Sam. Her breath smelled of licorice. Her upper arms pinned his fingers to the concrete ears.

"Ow!" they said together, and then Sam felt Darryl tugging at his legs. An instant later he felt some faint, yet profound shift in gravity. Someone else cried out behind them and the horse did a first slow-, then fast-motion topple forward, ending with an abrupt *clunk* as its front hooves kissed the pavement between Sam's legs.

Delft cried out and landed on her rear end on the gravel verge of the parking lot. Sam found himself on his knees, still clutching the horse's ears, as if trying to subdue it. Mr. Larose was already yelling his way across the parking lot.

Chapter 9

By Monday, Darryl had turned The Tipping of the Hoo Lee Horse into an epic performance piece in which he took center stage. In Darryl's telling, he was the first aboard, and he'd intended toppling all along. Beyond these outrageous lies, Sam caught a hint of ridicule in Darryl's impersonation of him.

"So I let go of him? And then Sam's like, *Whoaoaoaoaoh, save me,* as if he's falling off a cliff or something," Darryl would say, hitting the dirt to flop around helplessly. Then, leaping back up, he'd cradle his arms. "And I'm, like, trying to catch Delft so she doesn't hurt herself . . ." Yeah, right, Sam thought. He could imagine which parts of Delft Darryl had wanted to catch—as if she'd even needed catching. "And then Mr. Larose is running out at us, all yelling, 'You crazy kiiiiids!' "

At this point, Darryl would switch to jumping jacks to demonstrate adult frenzy. "And we're all like, *Let's get out of heeeeere!*" Arms and knees would pump to indicate running. "Except Sam's still lying in the dirt like he's *impaled* on the horse, so we all go back for him and he's like, *groaning,* and we get caught? So the horse got tipped," Darryl would gleefully conclude with a masterful if sudden return to his opening premise, "all because of me!"

By the fifth time he heard this, Sam had given up trying to correct details. They were in the music room after school, waiting for band practice to begin. As Darryl went into his windup, Sam wandered over to where an acoustic guitar sat on a stand. He hadn't told anyone he'd been trying to play one, mainly because he was such a rank beginner, but now he needed something, anything, to drown out Darryl, at least in his own ears. Besides, he was still feeling let down after this morning's conversation with Delft in the library.

Delft had been sitting in a study carrel when he approached her, busily writing something on flimsy blue paper. A letter, Sam guessed, because there was one of those red-and-blue-edged airmail envelopes on the desk as well. He didn't take the time to ask, because he wanted to get right to the heart of things. It had taken a lot of work to get back the courage he'd had on Friday night and he had the feeling it might slip away any second, leaving him red-faced and wordless. He'd gotten as far as, "Hey Delft? You remember that girl at St. Tiffany's you said who might—" when Delft briskly cut him off. Perhaps she was anxious to get back to her letter before the bell rang.

At any rate, she said, "I asked her already, Sam. She said she never heard of anybody named Manhattan."

"No, *Madison.*"

"Whatever. No singers with weird names. Sorry."

"That's okay. Thanks."

Once again the trail had gone cold. Now he looked at the guitar. Not having a crash helmet, maybe this would do to block things out. He plopped down on a stool, picked up the instrument, and felt his way through the five chords of "Hey Joe." When he had them, he called over to Darryl, "Hey Darryl, what Jimi Hendrix tune is this?" The answer wasn't the real point; Darryl, being Mr. Hendrix, would know it. The point was: *look at me; bet you didn't know I could play guitar, did you?*

"Wait," called Darryl, who was in the middle of trying to catch Delft. Sam started strumming anyway, fumbling a little, but gaining confidence as he went. He began to play louder, even attempting the little signature hammer-on on the E chord at the end of the cycle. Mr. Carnoostie came in, carrying some music.

Instinctively he began nodding his head to Sam's slightly ragged beat. As Darryl finished his story, Sam, still strumming, called over again.

"So Darryl, what tune is it?"

Darryl turned, saw Sam with the guitar, and straightened. His face went blank. His eyes flicked around the room. "I didn't hear it. Play it for me again."

Sam obliged, a little more nervously, now that he had listeners. Still, the progression of chords was recognizable. "Ummm," Darryl said. Everyone looked at him. He grinned. You could see he was more pleased about everyone looking at him than he was worried by not being able to name the song. Sam kept strumming.

"Come on, Darryl," Mr. Carnoostie kidded from across the room. "Even I know that one. 'Hey, Joe . . .' " He broke into a croaking rendition of the first line.

"Ooh," Darryl said, blankly. "I guess I didn't get it, the way Sam was playing it, out of time like that. I think maybe the real way is in a different key."

"Nope," Sam said. "That's the right key. I played it to the CD." Actually, his dad had played it to the CD, but if Darryl was going to weasel around . . .

Darryl made a puzzled face and changed tactics. "I dunno if I have that one, then."

"I thought you had a whole bunch of Hendrix." Sam couldn't resist rubbing it in. After all Darryl's blathering about Jimi Hendrix, he couldn't recognize one of his best-known songs?

"No, just one." Darryl busied himself fitting his clarinet together. "But it's the best one."

"Hey," said a grade twelve, coming over. "Can you show me those chords?"

Sam savored the victory. It was all he had to savor for the next while. By the time they walked home, Darryl was acting as if it had never happened and Sam had other things to occupy him.

"Wanta rent a movie tonight?" Darryl asked.

"I can't," Sam said with truthful regret. Despite Darryl's new ability to bug him, there were still times when he was fun, and Sam didn't like to turn down an invitation. Unfortunately, he had homework and an argument to have with his mom. "Don't you have homework?" he asked Darryl.

"Just a little." Darryl shrugged. At lunch today he'd been joking about a math test on which he'd scored seventeen percent. "Maybe I'll call Delft. Hey, what were you talking to her about anyway, when I pulled your legs?"

"I didn't say anything to her." Sam wasn't mentioning Madison Dakota to Darryl.

"Yeah, but you were going to. I heard you say, 'Hey Delft.' "

"Oh. Yeah. I wanted to ask her about this girl she knows at St. Tiffany's, Brooklyn or something."

"Why, is she hot?"

Sam shrugged. "I don't know. She just sounded interesting."

"Uh-huh," Darryl said, uninterested. "I think Delft really likes me. You should ask her, then we could all go out or something. Anyway, see ya. I gotta go."

Darryl trotted off, anxious to make his evening plans, leaving Sam mentally kicking himself. If Darryl mentioned the St. Tiffany's girl to Delft, she'd mention Madison Dakota to Darryl and Sam would never live it down. The question was, would Darryl be interested enough in anything that had to do with Sam instead of himself, to even remember to ask about it? For once, Sam hoped not.

The homework Sam had, while time-consuming, was the easy part of the evening. The argument with his mom, while short, was the hard part. The argument was all part of the fallout from Friday night. The penance for tipping a concrete horse at the Hoo Lee Garden was a lot steeper than Sam had expected. The horse had been too heavy for six inept teenagers and an excitable restaurant owner to put back into place, so Smitty had helped out next morning with a backhoe. For this, Sam owed Smitty two hours of leaf raking at J. Earl Goodenough's, even though Smitty had found the whole thing pretty funny. Then everybody had had to chip in with paint and labor on Saturday to repair the horses, which had gotten scuffed in all the action.

All of this was fair enough—the freight you paid for high school fame. What was totally unfair, as far as Sam was concerned, was that for his share of the paint, and on general principles, he also owed his mom as much work on her teen hangout petition as she deemed necessary.

"I'll work at the Bin for free," he'd plea-bargained. "Or ground me. Please!"

This had not worked. "You horse around, Sam"—Mrs. Foster had chuckled at her own joke—"you pay the price. I want kids signed up. I want adults."

"Like who?"

His mom had just happened to have a list. On Sunday, supposedly a day of rest, Sam had headed out, and he'd tried again today. Smitty and Ms. Broom had signed. Mr. Gernsbach signed, along with the other Stompers. Sam's Uncle Dave signed. Mr. Carnoostie signed. Amanda and Darryl and Larry and Steve and Janice and Delft, also horsers-around, signed. A few of the other kids Sam knew signed, but most couldn't have cared less, not being skids who liked to hang around Lint Lane—and Sam wasn't going to ask any of them. Nor was he going to ask the rest of the people on the list. The embarrassment potential was too high. This, he knew, was going to cause an argument.

Sure enough, his mom handed the petition back and the wrangling began. Finally, a compromise was reached. "The Goodenoughs and the Hoogstrattens and you're off the hook— except for coming to the town council meeting when we present."

The town council meeting he figured he could duck later. Sam dealt with the more pressing problem.

"But Delft already told me there's no way her parents will sign." This was true. Delft had said her dad didn't like the idea of a downtown hangout for teens at all.

"Well, that just makes it more of a challenge, doesn't it, dear?"

"Aw, Mom."

J. Earl. turned out to be easy. The great man was on his lawn again, dismantling his peeing-boy lawn statue for winter storage when Sam finally went by on Thursday afternoon. Pleading homework, Sam had put off the petition for as long as possible.

J. Earl had moved the little sprayer back out to the front yard, and it seemed to Sam that there was something different about it as he explained his visit. J. Earl drew in his intimidating eyebrows.

"So, you want me to sign something asking for a public space, right in the middle of town, for a bunch of yahoos to hang around in, to yell and play loud, stupid music and plot trouble?"

"I guess so," Sam admitted.

"Why not?" said J. Earl, seizing Sam's pen. "That should stir things up. Maybe it'll keep them away from here, too. My little buddy has unwanted visitors sometimes." He tilted his head, and Sam now noticed that a crucial portion of the lawn statue had been painted a bright purple. J. Earl completed his signature with a flourish, then glared up at Sam from beneath the hedgerow of his brow. "But I want a guarantee on the loud, stupid music. It'll drive Sidney Glebe nuts."

As he said this, a green Range Rover cruised past. Mrs. Felice Doberman was behind the wheel. As Sam and J. Earl looked her way, she returned her gaze to the road.

"Is she signing?" J. Earl asked. Mrs. Doberman was a force to be reckoned with in Hope Springs, and Sam knew J. Earl didn't like her. Apart from organizing the O. Sidney Glebe project, the party in his honor, and the Friends of Music, she also more or less ran the Royal Theater Restoration Committee, the Town Beautiful panel, and the annual House and Garden Tour. For complicated reasons, this last project had once caused Sam, J. Earl, Robin, Smitty, Darryl, and Ms. Broom to festoon her estate with all the cheesy lawn ornaments in town. Mrs. D. was not amused, and though her loathsome son was blamed, Sam had long suspected that *she* suspected him and J. Earl.

Now he said, "My mom asked her, but she said no."

"Excellent," said J. Earl, and signed again.

Sam then headed downtown, to Hoog's Blooms, the flower shop owned by Delft's parents. Lint Lane and the Bulging Bin were almost directly across the street. The door chimed as Sam stepped into a profusion of greenery, ornaments, baskets, and vases; the kind of artful clutter that always made someone Sam's size nervous. The chance to knock over something valuable seemed to lurk behind every leaf. The shop was also warm and humid. This was part of the reason that Sam instantly broke out in a sweat. The other reason was that Delft's dad was behind the counter, right by the door.

Bert "Hoog" Hoogstratten was a ruddy-cheeked man with half-glasses on a finder string, Abe Lincoln chin whiskers, and arms the size of Manitoba. He was primping a generous spray of white and lavender blooms in a tall, white vase. Country music twanged softly in the background hush. Mr. Hoogstratten hummed tunelessly along. Nestled in the midst of the flowers an oval placard read *With Deepest Sympathy.* A funeral. Sam sweated some more; maybe he should come back on a less solemn occasion.

Mr. Hoogstratten, however, gave a final cheery flick to some greenery and cried out, "Yas, sir?" with the faintest trace of a Dutch accent. His smile morphed into something closer to lip-pursing as his above-the-glasses gaze focused on Sam and identified the species *genus teenus.*

"Um, hi, Mr. Hoogstratten. I'm Sam Foster. I'm a friend of Delft's?"

"Delft?" The lip-pursing descended into a frown. "How do you know my daughter?"

"Well, we go to the High together?"

"Go get HIGH together?" Mr. Hoogstratten suddenly loomed like Manitoba and Saskatchewan combined. Sam shrank back.

"No! The *high* school," he corrected quickly. "Hope Springs High."

"Ohhh, yah. At da high school." Mr. Hoogstratten resettled himself.

"Yeah." Sam found himself a little breathless. "My mom runs the Bulging Bin?"

"Ohh." The frown receded to lip-pursing. "Your mom is a very nice lady," said Mr. Hoogstratten formally. "I know her from the Business Association. Shirley."

"Um, Shelley, actually. Anyway, like, she's got this petition about getting the kids out from Lint Lane—"

"Excellent!" boomed Mr. Hoogstratten, as a different country number insinuated itself in behind him. "I'm glad your mom changed her mind. Those damn kids hanging around all the time, they're nothing but trouble. Last night, I swear to God, they spit all over my window after I closed. What am I going to do about something like that?" Mr. Hoogstratten scrabbled up a pen from a holder beside the cash. "Let 'em get a job, they got so much time on their hands. That's what I say."

He gestured for Sam to hand him the petition. Chuckling, he said, "I thought maybe you were one of them when you first came in. You don't get teenage business except Mother's Day and Valentine's. But now I know you're Shirley's son . . ."

"Oh, yeah, well," Sam said meaninglessly, so relieved he didn't bother about the name correction. He handed over the sheet of paper. "My mom says once they have their own space—"

"Yah, on a work farm," grunted Mr. Hoogstratten, adjusting his glasses on his nose.

"Well, actually my mom says it'd be that parking lot just over by—"

"WHAT?" Mr. Hoogstratten's eyes shot up over his glasses and his Lincoln beard seemed to quiver. "Not that again. What is this, some kind of a trick? I want them out, not down the street in some other eyesore! That's not what I pay my taxes for. No way, no sir!" He dropped the petition and slapped the countertop so hard the floral arrangement for the funeral did a little hop. Mr.

Hoogstratten caught the vase with one meaty hand. Sam could imagine it clenched around his neck. "You tell your mother I'll fight this tooth and nail."

Sam snagged the petition and began to back out of the store.

"And watch out for that planter!" snapped Mr. Hoogstratten. Sam swerved to avoid it. "And don't get my Delft involved in this!" He pushed open the door and escaped to cool October air as a female voice softly wailed, *"My heart's in a heat wave over you."* The door chimed shut as Mr. Hoogstratten cried, "Say, weren't you one of those horse kids?"

Across the street a skid was attempting to crush a pop tin on a friend's forehead. It wasn't until he was in the Bulging Bin that Sam realized the singer had been Madison Dakota.

Chapter 10

On Friday morning, Sam found himself summoned to the music room after announcements. The week was all but over and Darryl still hadn't said a word about Madison Dakota, even though he claimed to have talked to Delft on the phone every evening. This was fine with Sam. Maybe the danger was past.

At first it had seemed odd that Mr. Hoogstratten had a Madison Dakota CD and Delft couldn't even keep her name straight. On second thought, though, it had seemed normal. Delft had no interest in country music, he knew, any more than he was interested in the Dixieland portion of his own dad's CD collection—or much of the rest of it, either. Okay, Hendrix had been cool, and one or two others, but the rest, mercifully, was a blur: geezer music.

Speaking of which. Slouching into the music room, he found Darryl, Amanda, Larry, and twenty or so other fellow slouchers, all music students at the high school. Mr. Carnoostie, more inflated than ever, was bustling about a figure Sam recognized. O. Sidney Glebe had arrived for his workshop.

Glebe was again dressed in black. As Mr. Carnoostie introduced him, he stood listening, head tilted to one side, his posture suggesting an elongated S. Then, with a lengthy hand, he slowly pinched his nose, a gesture that ended with his thumb beneath his silvery chin, his middle finger sprawled along his upper lip, and his index finger stretching up his cheek, pointing toward his rather knobby temple.

In this pose he silently regarded everyone. Then he tilted back his head for a nostril-widening breath and removed his hand to form a loosely clenched fist, which he held at chest level.

"Right. Thank you," drawled O. Sidney Glebe, in response to Mr. Carnoostie's introduction, or perhaps to applause that only he heard. "Today I'd like you to do some listening with me." He paused. "Also to do some thinking about how we listen and what we listen to. Now, first, I'd like you to take your chairs and arrange them in a semicircle around the room." He gestured languidly with his fist. "And do it quietly, please." His voice was as mild as his gesture, but then it didn't need to be anything else. No matter what was going to happen with O. Sidney Glebe, it had to be better than French. Or math. Or history. Or getting signatures on a petition. At first, anyway.

Everyone looked at each other, then rose in a babble of conversation, scraping and clanking their chairs.

"Hey, HEY!" A very different Glebe voice arced over the clatter. His hand was still before his chest. A jaw muscle flickered as he waited for silence. "I said *quietly*. Try it again, please."

Everyone moved more carefully. Glebe waited. In the rearrangement, Sam found himself between Amanda and Robert Goodwood, a grade eleven who played first trumpet in the band and who dressed far too neatly to be normal. Robert also got high marks, and his still-unbroken voice was featured in a local choir. These things did not help around the school, where he was ranked lowest of the low: a gay/weird, browner band nerd. Sam edged closer to Amanda.

Glebe asked, "Does anyone remember the first words in the Bible?"

Robert's hand went up. That was another thing: his regular church attendance also classified him as a water-walker. Robert said, " 'In the beginning, God created the heaven and the earth.' "

" 'And the earth was without form,' " Glebe continued, " 'and darkness was on the face of the deep. And the spirit of God moved

upon the face of the waters. And God said, "Let there be light." ' "
Another pause, then Glebe asked: "What came first, sound or light?"

Robert's hand again; the only hand, in fact. No one else, including Sam, was quite sure what this was about—the Bible in music class—or what to make of O. Sidney Glebe.

"Sound," said Robert, lisping.

"Thank you," said Glebe. "In the story of creation, the first story we have, sound comes even before light. 'And the spirit of God moved upon the face of the waters. And God said . . . ' " Glebe eyed them over his beaky nose. "What did God's voice sound like?"

Silence, except for some rustling. Kids glanced at each other; someone snickered. "Like Mr. Carnoostie," came a voice. Kids laughed.

Glebe chuckled. "Or J. Earl Goodenough," he said. "With him there's *always* sound well before the light comes on."

This got a tepid response, few teens being watchers of the national news. Sam laughed and immediately felt a little guilty. Glebe glanced at him, then said, "No, I think of God's voice this way." He walked over to a black case Sam remembered all too well. Glebe extracted a monstrous tuning fork, rapped it on Mr. Carnoostie's desk, and touched the ball end to the blackboard. A deep hum suffused the room. "A vibration," said O. Sidney Glebe. He turned and cocked an eyebrow at Sam, who felt himself blushing mightily. "Pure sound. From it comes darkness and light."

He turned to the classroom piano and rapped out a familiar phrase that ended in dramatic bass notes. "Who knows that?"

More hands this time, from movie buffs. "It's from *2001*."

Glebe nodded. "*Also Sprach Zarathustra*. Richard Strauss. That first part was darkness. This next part is light." He played the next phrase with its two ascending notes at the end. "Then they're combined in creation. Unity." He played the triumphant resolution, then turned back to the class. "Strauss was interested in Zoroastrianism." He chatted for a moment about Plato and the Zoroastrians, as if they were an eccentric bunch living just outside of town. "And Strauss encodes it all in sound, in vibrations."

Sam listened; everyone did—although, Sam could tell, with differing amounts of understanding and/or patience. Sam wasn't sure how much of this he got himself. For all his mild manner, O. Sidney Glebe was like the optional endless-ammo machine gun you could earn in the *WMD: Search and Destroy* video game, firing out ideas so fast and odd that you couldn't relax. Sam wondered if university was like this.

Before he could decide, Glebe abruptly said, "Now. I'm going to give each of you a number. Remember it. One, two, three, four, one, two . . ." He counted off around the semicircle. "Ones make this noise with me: Wowowowowow. Twos: Eepeeepeeeepeeeep. Threes: Blub. Blub. Blub. Fours: Ooo. Ooo. Ooo.

"All right, spread out around the room. Get away from your like numbers and sounds. Close your eyes. When I say go, everyone start making your sound and keep making it. As you do, move around the room and try to join up with others making the same sound until you're in four groups. Ready? Go."

They tried it several times, Glebe changing the objectives on each go-round. Bumping into people proved to be unavoidable.

"Oh man," Darryl whispered. "I sure wish Delft was here." Then, "Oh well, maybe I can bump into *her* instead." He nodded at an over-endowed grade eleven several inches taller than he was. You had to give him credit for trying. Sam wandered, blub-blubbing self-consciously and thinking of Madison Dakota. He managed only to bump into Robert.

They spent the rest of the day in equally odd ways. Did train whistles sound more than one note at a time? Yes. What were the notes? The E-flat minor chord. What pattern of longs and shorts did they blow at a crossing? They cataloged all the sounds they heard as Glebe wound up and pitched a crumpled sheet of paper against the blackboard. They tried to remember the first sound they had heard that morning. Sam wasn't sure he got it all, but it was interesting, he had to admit—to himself, anyway. Other kids looked befuddled or bored. No one, however, seemed up to giving the maestro a hard time. Glebe, Sam thought, would have made one scary supply teacher.

Finally they were split into groups of three and given a sheet of paper. On it, in a circular pattern, were printed an empty rectangle, a jagged line, a huge black dot, a spiral, and the kind of cartoon swoosh lines that indicated something speeding through the air. Sam looked blankly at his paper with his partners, Amanda and Robert. Glebe leaned against the back of a chair, his loose fist aloft once again.

"Now, I'll be back to see you later in the year. When I return, I expect you to have two things for me. One, your group's opinion as to this question: What *is* music? And two, your group is to orchestrate and be ready to perform the score I've just given you. You may use any instruments you wish or anything for an instrument. Any questions?"

A grade twelve raised her hand. "But these aren't notes or anything."

Glebe nodded. "Not traditional ones. But if symbols suggest sounds to you, they're a score. What kind of sound would that black dot be? How would you make it?"

Sam, puzzling this out, was annoyed to notice Robert nodding sagely. He sensed this was not going to be a dream partnership.

"Now"—Glebe stood up straight—"we'll wrap up with a sound walk. I'll lead. I want you to walk in single file, with at least six paces between each of you, in total silence. Listen for and remember as many sounds as you can. When we get to the far side of the playing field, we'll regroup and talk. Let's go."

It was an Indian summer afternoon. Pacing dutifully through the weeds that grew around the perimeter of the running track, Sam noted his own footsteps, banging from the sheet metal shop, the wind in his ears, a train whistle, the faint swish of traffic on the highway. He tried to listen to them one at a time. Concentrating hard, it took him a moment to realize that Amanda was gesturing to him, hopping from foot to foot and pointing down. Farther ahead, Glebe paced calmly on, his face to the sky, nostrils no doubt wider than ever. Sam looked quizzically back at Amanda. Screwing up her face, she pointed down again. Sam looked at his sneakered feet in a patch of weeds. He shrugged back.

"For God's sake," Amanda yelled in frustration, "he's led us through a patch of poison ivy."

It was perhaps the most significant sound of the day. Heads snapped around. Scratching followed.

Chapter 11

Robin, home for the weekend, thought the poison ivy was a riot. "Did he get it too?" she asked, meaning O. Sidney Glebe.

Sam, who had itchy ankles—he and Darryl had been wearing shorts, despite it being October (there was a kid, now in grade eleven, who had made Hope Springs history by wearing shorts all year in tenth grade)—did not think the poison ivy was a riot. He flopped on the couch and tried not to scratch. "I dunno if he got it or not. He acted too cool to show."

"So was he cool?"

Sam looked at the red welts on his leg. O. Sidney Glebe had a style, all right. Whether it was cool was hard to say.

"You should have gotten him to sign your petition."

Sam rolled his eyes and made a shushing motion at his sister. He'd had enough trouble with the petition. It was no use. From the kitchen, where their dad was doing something menacing to tofu, their mom called, "He wouldn't count—he's not a resident." She stepped into the doorway, holding a sheaf of papers. "Anyway, we've got enough signatures here—if we have a good presentation to council on Tuesday, particularly from our teen reps, of which Sam is one."

"*What?*" Sam sat up on the couch. He'd forgotten that part.

"Don't worry, dear. You just have to be there. Amanda's doing the talking."

The council chamber was on the second floor of the Hope Springs town hall, a domed Victorian pile across the street from the band shell. When Sam entered with his mom's group Tuesday evening, the first thing he saw was a line of geezers along a long table at the front, nodding over their double-double coffees from Donut Deelite. These, he gathered, were the councilors. Facing them, in the public seats, were a group of adults looking grumpy but not as geezerish. Mr. Hoogstratten, looking the grumpiest, sat in the forefront. Sam sensed this was not the time to ask him where he had gotten a Madison Dakota CD. Gliding around, chatting graciously, was Mrs. Doberman. There were no skids, despite the notice about the meeting that Mrs. Foster had posted in Lint Lane. For that matter, there was no Madison Dakota either. Sam figured the odds on either showing up were about the same.

Sam slouched as deeply as he could into a chair beside Amanda, who sat up straight. His mom's group also included a minister, two high school teachers (the guidance counselor and Mr. Foster), and a couple of other downtown business owners, including Amanda's dad, who owned Grandstand Sports and Collectibles. Mrs. Foster had the petition. As they waited for the meeting to begin, Sam bent to his still-itchy ankles.

"Don't scratch," reminded Mrs. Foster out of one side of her mouth, then smiling with the other as she smoothly changed gears to greet Mrs. Doberman. "Why hello, Felice. How nice to see you! Here for our big meeting, are you?"

"Oh, just a little Friends of Music business for afterward," drawled Mrs. Doberman. "Speaking of which, I believe that's Sydney Glebe. Whatever is he doing here? I must say hello. Have you met him?"

"No, but Sam has."

"Has he? Oh, at the high school, I suppose. Apparently Sydney did something just super over there."

"I think he met him elsewhere as well."

Sam slouched deeper and beamed *please shut up* thought waves at his mom.

"I wonder where."

Before his mom could say, Mrs. Doberman went on, "Anyway, I'll introduce you sometime. Must fly. Good luck."

Sam, relieved, watched her hasten to the back of the room. Sure enough, the composer was there, holding the small black object he'd had at the fair. He saw Sam looking at him and bestowed a nod of recognition. Sam felt himself blush again. He sputtered a nod back as Glebe rose to greet Mrs. Doberman. At the same instant, Sam heard someone settle into the chair beside him. He turned to see J. Earl Goodenough.

"There better be fireworks," said the great man. "I pay enough taxes for them."

The mayor called the meeting to order and began to run through its regular business. An *Eternal* reporter bustled in and O. Sidney Glebe sauntered out. He and J. Earl nodded stiffly at one another.

"He really get that helmet off your head?" J. Earl more or less whispered. Sam nodded. "Well, just be careful. The man's a total whacko, you know."

Sam didn't know, but right now he didn't have time to find out. New business, announced the mayor. As chairperson, he recognized Mrs. Shelley Foster.

Sam's mom carried the petition up to the small speaker's table and adjusted the microphone. She began describing the problem in Lint Lane and explaining why turning the little-used parking lot up the street into a teen space would be the best and cheapest solution. Sam didn't listen; he'd heard it all at home. He sank more deeply in his chair, trying to ignore the itch in his ankles and his worries about helping in the presentation. Thank God Amanda was going to do all the talking. She glanced at him and grinned, rolling her eyes slightly.

"Why are we *doing* this?" he'd muttered to her as they'd climbed the stairs to the council chamber. "This is so dumb." Which was true. You couldn't get skids to go someplace, just by giving them a space, unless you used some kind of tricky reverse psychology, like Sam had tried with his earphones and Steffi. And look how that had worked out. The whole point about skids was that they'd go wherever you didn't want them; even adults should have known that. Amanda, a step ahead as always, had cut to the real point.

"Because we tipped over a horse, remember? And I want to apply to the recreation department for a summer job next year, so this will make me look good. And, well, you know, I get to do it with someone I like."

Sam sat up and forgot his itch. Because someone she liked . . . ? Did that mean him? Did that mean *like* like? Had she really said *that?* He looked at Amanda again. She was leaning forward, listening to the arguments, pro and con, being volleyed around the council chamber. She'd been nice to him on the weekend, too, calling to say Delft hoped everybody came to the movies, because Darryl had invited her and said everyone was going but then had somehow forgotten to invite anyone else. In fact, she was always nice to him. But saying what she said was like saying, well . . . Ho-lee. But here he was with his heart belonging to a mystery girl. Or should it any longer? How long could he feel *Lost* for a girl who might as well not exist?

Mrs. Stewart said she was local and Mr. Hoogstratten had her CD, but the truth was Sam couldn't even picture her face. (What with hat, curls, makeup, and microphone, it had been hard to see her face—unlike, say, her navel, or other neck-down-type things.) Sam pushed thoughts of these from his mind. What should he feel for Amanda? That was the question right now. She was pretty, not to mention ridiculously smart and way better than Sam at sports. They had kind of liked each other that way in grade six. But now they were just friends, right? *Right?* Life was suddenly complicated, even leaving out homework and the fact that Amanda was waving her hand to speak and even now standing up. Standing up! That meant—around him, the others were nudging him and whispering, "Hurry up, Sam! It's your turn, stand up!"

He stood up.

Amanda, supported by Sam, was supposed to make the last plea on behalf of kids, for grade-A emotional impact. Then the council was supposed to vote. Mrs. Foster had done her best to organize this as well. She'd been chatting up councilors, buttonholing them when they came into the store, calling them at home, using connections that only a lifelong Hope Springer could have. By her tally almost half were on side, with several waffling.

Amanda was already at the speaker's table. Sam hurried after her, attempting the Survival Slouch at the same time. Hurried Survival was hard to do. He stubbed a size-eleven foot into the carpet. His itching ankle whacked the table leg.

It felt as if his poison ivy had caught fire. Sam gasped and bent to clutch his leg. His head hit the microphone. The resultant CLONK and "Owww!" were so loud that even a councilor having an after-dinner nap sat up to attention.

Sam spent the rest of Amanda's presentation rubbing his forehead and trying not to rub his leg. He didn't hear a word she said. As he stumbled back to his seat, he did hear the mayor say, "The chair recognizes Felice Doberman."

"Less than smooth, Foster," J. Earl growled as Sam sat down. Sam scowled. Mrs. Doberman's voice was already filling the room.

"Mr. Chairman, I came to speak for Friends of Music tonight, but I feel I have to make a suggestion here, too, because I suddenly see the two topics are related." She smiled benignly. "Young Sam's little mishap just now—are you all right there, dear?" She turned in Sam's direction. Sam blushed furiously and nodded. "Sam's mishap suggested to me what I'm afraid is a major flaw in this teen space idea: liability. Now Sam and Amanda here are obviously intelligent, motivated, civic-minded teens—"

"Just not very coordinated," whispered J. Earl. Sam, still blushing, went into the deepest Survival Slouch of his career. He didn't dare look at Amanda.

"—who you are not going to find loitering on street corners," continued Mrs. Doberman. "They take responsibility for themselves.

But there are others who do not. If someone like Sam has an accident, he knows it's probably his own fault. But some of the young people who tend to be, shall we say, disruptive down along Lint Lane clearly take no responsibility for anything. If one of them were to fall off a skateboard and break a leg at a town-sanctioned venue, there could be lawsuits galore. The insurance costs would be prohibitive; the town couldn't afford them."

The councilors stirred like the sludge at the bottom of their double-doubles. Eyebrows knit, sore bottoms were eased from chair seats, deep breaths were taken. Several even picked up their pens, then put them down again. Mr. Hoogstratten's group nodded vigorously. A couple applauded. Meanwhile, Sam felt a ripple of alarm pass through the people around him. His mom sat bolt upright, listening intently. Sam was too busy trying to figure out whether he'd just been insulted by Mrs. Doberman.

Mrs. Doberman continued. "So, on behalf of Friends of Music, I have a compromise suggestion. We've been thinking about this for some time. The Friends will pay half the cost of installing outdoor speakers and piping classical music into the Lint Lane/downtown area as part of our Beautiful Town Beautiful Music project, if the Downtown Business Association and the town will pick up the other half. Compared to a teen space, it would be inexpensive. Plus, everyone could enjoy lovely music as part of the ambience, and for the young people in Lint Lane it would be a valuable addition to their music education. On the other hand," she paused and smiled blandly, "if it wasn't to their taste, they could always go elsewhere. Away from downtown, if necessary."

A rumble of approval swelled as Mr. Hoogstratten and company grasped the implication. Mrs. Foster sat stone-faced.

"I know this has been tried with great success in several communities, where they've discovered that young people for some reason had a particular problem with Mozart. Still, they've continued to play it, because, of course, eventually the kids will realize that this is in fact *for* them. And I say bravo to that. In the meantime of course, they can go wherever they choose. It's a free country."

There was another burst of applause. "We're toast, Foster," sighed J. Earl.

He was right. Despite Mrs. Foster's lobbying, the Hope Springs town council approved Mrs. Doberman's suggestion unanimously.

Mrs. Foster accepted defeat gamely, smiling to Mrs. Doberman, who repeated, "At the end of the day, Shelley, it's for the kids. It really is."

Sam looked for Amanda. She'd been swept away in the tide of people exiting the council chamber. Slowly, he followed his parents downstairs and outside. Across the street Amanda was getting into the car with her dad. She smiled and waved. Sam waved cautiously back. He became aware that J. Earl was standing on the town hall steps beside them, a checkered cloth cap covering his bald dome.

"Don't worry about it," J. Earl was advising Sam's mom, " 'To strive, to seek, to find, / And not to yield,' " he quoted, adding, "Hang tough."

Mrs. Foster was more succinct. "For the kids, my ass," she said. Sam was shocked.

Chapter 12

O ver the next couple of weeks, O. Sidney Glebe drifted around town, Madison Dakota remained invisible, Darryl hovered around Delft like an oversized hummingbird (Sam, uncharitably, thought his ears added to the effect), and Amanda kept her distance. Perhaps this was because she was embarrassed, and waiting for Sam to say something back. Perhaps she couldn't believe she'd said something like that to a guy who'd then slam his head into a microphone. Perhaps she hadn't meant what Sam thought (though he was pretty sure she did). Or maybe, like everyone, she was so burdened with schoolwork there was no time for anything else—except working at her dad's store. The pre-Christmas retail steamroller was picking up speed.

Sam knew the feeling. He was sweeping in the Bulging Bin and fretting over his love life—if it existed—when Glebe strolled in on a November Saturday afternoon. Sam was thinking that there were advantages to being *Lost* over someone you'd never met— namely, that you couldn't do the wrong thing. Maybe this was why he'd never gone back to ask Mr. Hoogstratten about the CD. At first, he'd told himself he was waiting for things to cool down after the petition upset. Now he was telling himself he was just too busy and too confused over Amanda. *Really,* a voice inside was nagging, *you're just too chicken.*

Trying to ignore the voice, he snagged a chocolate kiss and several coffee beans with the opposite edges of the broom, a superior move, as Glebe asked, "How long has *Eine Kleine Nachtmusik* been playing out there?"

"Ever since they found out it drove away kids." Sam caught his mom's flat reply as well. She outlined the controversy, which Glebe had not stayed to hear about at the council meeting. Sam stopped and headed his broom back the other way. This was not the first time he'd heard his mom have a conversation like this. He wished it would be the last.

Speakers had indeed blossomed under the eaves of various businesses around the lane and the Four Corners. When Sam first heard the music, he'd been overstressed by term tests, a geography project, and a science report, not to mention Glebe's assignment, which no one had even started. For one horrible moment he'd thought that he had his CD earphones on and something had gone wrong with *Drop Zone,* the newest offering by Recycled Lepers, a hot retro, rap-metal, ska, punk band.

Since the fair, just the thought of earphones had been scary, so learning that the music was everywhere had been a relief. It wasn't now: Sam often liked to think of his life as a movie, but not with Mozart on the soundtrack.

Sam slalomed his broom down the other aisle. Glebe said, "But I notice you have classical music playing in here."

"True," admitted Mrs. Foster, "but it's my store, not a public place. You don't have to come in; I'm not inflicting it on you. That street is for everyone. And now look at it: no kids. Where do they go?"

The answer, Sam knew, was Jimmy's Pizza, just around the corner on John Street. If you bought a slice, Jimmy let you hang out as long as you wanted. Which was good, because when it got busy and Jimmy started to sweat, you could watch his hairpiece slide around. Sam had heard about this from Robin and had even witnessed it himself once. Most of the time, though, Jimmy's was Skid City, so he didn't go there a lot.

Sam kept his mouth shut. As he reached the front of the store, he went into Survival Slouch. "'Scuse me." He spun the broom a little too fast. The chocolate kiss snicked across the floor and caromed off Glebe's black-shod toe. "Sorry." Sam went deeper into slouch mode. Retrieving the kiss, he managed to sweep a layer of cornstarch onto the man's shoe. *"Sorry."*

"Don't mention it." Glebe lifted his foot a few inches and shook it gently. "It's Sam, isn't it?" He still had one foot off the ground. "Actually, I came to see you."

Glebe put the foot down. Sam looked up. "Mrs. Goodenough," Glebe said as he tilted his head aristocratically, "said you might be the person to do some work for me, if it's all right with your parents."

"Fire away," said Mrs. Foster.

"Well, as you know," said Glebe, "Mrs. Doberman, via the Friends of Music, is paying me to compose a piece about the town. For that I need sounds from it." He took from his coat pocket the black object Sam had seen before. "This is a digital micro-cassette recorder with a built-in microphone; quite sensitive. The sound reproduction is surprisingly good. I've been recording things around town, but I'm going away for some weeks, until after Christmas. You seem to be a person who gets around, so I'm wondering if you'd care to carry on taping for me—for pay, of course, and a credit on the program."

"What kinds of stuff would you want me to tape?" Sam asked, intrigued.

"Anything that's part of this town. Sounds, voices—from as many different places and times as possible. They can be long or short; I'll edit what I use later. Just identify where and when you taped it."

Sam looked at his mom. She smiled and shrugged. "Sure," he said. "Cool." And it was. This was way better than helping at the demo derby, cooler even than putting lawn ornaments all over the Doberman place. This was professional music. Darryl couldn't top this in a million years. In fact, he thought meanly, maybe he wouldn't tell Darryl. Instead he'd invite all his *friends* to come taping with him. Gee, didn't I tell you, Darryl, he'd say, I must have forgot. We had a *great* time, too.

Glebe showed Sam how to operate the recorder while listening through a small earpiece. Sam gingerly put it in his ear and pressed RECORD. Through the earpiece he heard with great clarity the *bong* as the door of the Bin opened. He turned—*rustle rustle*—to see Robert Goodwood enter and make for the bulk snacks. Sam pressed STOP.

"You'll learn how to keep yourself quiet while it's running," Glebe said. "And try to keep it inconspicuous." He showed Sam the other function buttons.

Sam nodded as Robert approached the cash. He had an assortment of snack foods in bags, all small portions.

"Can't make up your mind there, Robert?" Mrs. Foster teased gently.

"Oh, yes, Mrs. Foster," said Robert seriously. "I can. I chose these on purpose"—he gave Glebe a sidelong glance—"for their sounds."

Glebe in turn gave Sam a look that flicked down to the digital recorder. Sam pressed RECORD.

"That's very interesting," the composer said. "You choose food for its sound."

"Yes sir," Robert said eagerly. "As a private project, I've been trying to orchestrate that score you gave us entirely to nutritious snacks. Listen." Chewing vigorously, he proceeded to demonstrate the sonic differences between trail mix and banana softees. Sam heard first some muffled crunching and then not much of anything.

"I'm not hearing a lot," Glebe said gravely, in listening posture.

Robert swallowed and nodded. "That's the only problem. *I* can hear it beautifully, but I have to find a way to amplify it. Those banana things are exactly right for the wavy lines part; the way they stretch and stick to your teeth."

"Getting the music out of your head and into the world can be a problem," Glebe agreed. "I wish you luck."

"One of our best musicians," Mrs. Foster said as Robert left the store.

"Also nuttier than a fruitcake," Glebe said, handing Sam extra tapes and preparing to leave himself. He stopped at the door. "Of course, people have called *me* a total whacko as well." He looked at Sam. "Thank you. I'll be in touch."

With that, he followed his nose out the door.

Chapter 13

Sam already knew one thing he wanted to record. When his shift ended at two, he made a beeline for home and the first ADHD practice in three weeks. With no Madison Dakota to form a new band, Sam had stuck with the old one, while noodling with the guitar on the side. Once in a while it even seemed as if they were getting better. Maybe a tape would give him the answer.

Larry and Darryl were already waiting on the porch, shuffling in the cold. Sam let them in (his dad being at a Stompers practice) and they headed for the basement. An hour later, as they passed the earpiece around listening to the playback, Sam couldn't help but wonder why he'd been in such a hurry.

"Really, it could be just a recording balance thing," Darryl said. "Like, this is kind of an ambient mike, right? What we need is a bunch of—"

"It's *ambient,*" Larry interrupted, "and we still totally bite."

Sam glumly nodded his agreement. Glebe had asked what music was. Sam didn't know the answer, except that it wasn't this.

"Maybe we should take a break for a while," he suggested, instead of saying, "Yeah. I quit." He didn't want to sound as if he was wimping out.

To his surprise, the others brightened considerably.

"I think so too," said Larry. "I've got so much studying right now—"

"Yeah," Darryl chimed in. "Me too." *Yeah, right,* Sam thought. Last week, Darryl had been waving around the worst midterm report of anybody, acting as if he was proud of how bad it was. He went on, "And I think I'm gonna be busy with *other things.*"

His deliberate emphasis on "other things" meant Delft. That was what it had meant for ages now, though as far as anyone knew they had never gone out as a couple.

"Yeah, I'm pretty sure Delft wants to go out with me now," Darryl said nonchalantly, packing up his guitar. "So I'm going to ask her out on a date. I've been waiting for the right time? And then when I have a girlfriend and stuff, see, I'm not going to have time to practice."

"When are you going to ask her?" Larry wanted to know. He kept a straight face. Rumor had it that Darryl had been bombarding Delft with invitations that were always turned down.

Darryl had extensive plans for the asking-out. He proceeded to share them. Larry smirked, but Sam didn't. For once, he was in sympathy with Darryl. He had his own case of the hesitation blues over girls at the moment, and a surprisingly downbeat feeling about the end of ADHD. What had he done? Maybe they'd stunk, but they'd been a band. Now he was going to have to find something else. More than ever, Madison Dakota seemed like the key to everything. More than ever, she seemed as distant as summer.

Larry and Darryl clunked their amps and instrument cases up the basement steps. Sam followed, feeling empty and sad. Mr. Foster, back from his own practice, was at the kitchen table, a bottle of beer in front of him, his jacket slung over the back of his chair and his feet on his euphonium case. Over the last month or two Sam had grown more used to his being at school, where he now thought of him as Drama Dad. At home, of course, he hadn't changed at all.

"Well, how'd it go?" he asked as Sam closed the door on ADHD.

"We broke up."

"No kidding. So did we." His dad tipped back his beer.

"Really?" Sam was stunned. "The Stompers broke up?" His dad had played with them for as long as Sam could remember.

"Well, I quit actually. And it turned out a few of the other guys felt the same way, but no one had wanted to say so."

"But why?" For some reason his dad's news made Sam even more depressed. The Hope Springs Society Stompers were something that had always been, and he'd expected them to continue to be. Besides, his dad never liked it when Sam quit anything.

"It was old, Sam. I did it for ten years—it was making *me* old. I mean, God, I'm forty-six, playing music from thirty years before I was born. That makes me a musical seventy-six-year-old. Too old to rock and roll, too young to die. No thanks. I want to play stuff more contemporary, relevant, happening. You know?"

Sam nodded. "You mean like Aggressive Microwaves, Distempered Puppies?"

"Wellll . . ." Mr. Foster had some more beer. "I was thinking more of the kind of stuff I grew up with."

"But that's so old!"

"Thanks, Sam. Thanks a lot." His dad regarded him sourly over the rim of the bottle. Then he put his feet to the floor and stood up. "How about pizza tonight? Pepperoni okay?"

"You're not going to cook?"

"Just between you and me, I'm sick of cooking. Where shall we order from?"

"Antonio's."

Mr. Foster strolled over and pulled down the phonebook. Something jangled on his wrist. Something new. Sam stared at two shiny metal bracelets resting against a hemp watchband. His dad turned to the counter to flip the pages. Nestled at the base of his father's skull, secured by one of Robin's hair elastics, was what appeared to be the beginning of a ponytail. Sam swallowed in disbelief. Where had *that* come from? How long had . . . ?

"Here it is." Mr. Foster interrupted his amazement, punching numbers into the phone. "What are you doing tonight?" he asked as he waited for Antonio's to pick up.

"Studying, I guess."

"On a Saturday night? Geez, Sam, grade nine isn't *that* hard. Let's get a movie . . . Yes, I'd like to order for takeout please . . ."

For a moment the kitchen floor seemed to sway gently beneath Sam's feet, a mild enough sensation given that the world was turning upside down. When the feeling passed he headed for the basement to get the digital recorder. If the world *was* turning upside down, he might as well get it on tape.

Chapter 14

As it turned out, the world managed only to tilt before everyday life rushed back in like a winter wind. Mrs. Foster returned from the Bin and took the demise of the Stompers in stride. She didn't say a word about the bracelets or the ponytail. Had she seen them before? Why the heck hadn't he? Of course, who expected their folks to change? Sam wished Robin was around to whisper about this with. Then Steve called, inviting Sam to hang out with a bunch of the others that night and allowing Sam to escape watching *The Commitments* with his dad.

Sunday, he studied all day and plunked at the guitar on breaks. His confidence was coming back. On Monday, posters went up around the High advertising a Christmas video dance at the end of exams. On Wednesday, Mrs. Goldenrod, their English teacher, handed out copies of a J. Earl Goodenough book everyone was assigned to read over the holidays, then nailed the class with a surprise grammar quiz. On Thursday, exams began, and on Friday, Sam's mom reminded him that Saturday afternoon he and his friends were decorating an artificial Christmas tree for a charity raffle in return for community service hours.

Every student at Hope Springs High had to put in forty hours of community service before graduation. Sam had already notched two hours for helping at the demolition derby and another three for his sterling efforts on the petition and the town council meeting. Since he had another three and two-thirds years to get the rest of his hours, and adults seemed to be taking up way too much of his time lately, he was not pleased. Naturally, he didn't say this. Instead he said, "But what about exams? I have to study."

"Then get up early and study all morning," suggested his practical-minded mom. "You'll need a break by afternoon. I'll credit everyone with two hours, but the more friends you get to help, the less time it'll actually take."

Sam knew that a suggestion from his mom was the same as an order, so he salvaged what he could.

"Okay, but we get to decorate it any way we want."

"Complete artistic control," promised Mrs. Foster. "Just use things from the store." So much for Sam's vision of a Tree of Rock.

The raffle was in aid of the town food bank. Businesses and community groups were decorating theme Christmas trees that Handy Hardware was providing. Anyone could buy tickets to enter draws to win trees they liked. The decorated trees would be on display downtown for a week. So, on Saturday afternoon, Sam and his friends found themselves standing around a naked artificial Christmas tree in the shadowy auditorium of the Royal Theater. It was the first time they'd all been together in quite a while. Darryl, naturally, glued himself to Delft, except for time-outs clowning on the stepladder. Amanda showed up late and said she could only stay for a while before going back to her dad's store.

"I didn't want to miss it, though," she said to Sam, smiling and unzipping her coat. Did that mean because he was involved? He didn't have much time to wonder. Ever-practical, Amanda was already at work opening boxes.

The Royal was a sad and shabby relic of the nineteen-twenties. Restoring it to its former glory was another pet project of Mrs. Doberman's. Just now, she was overseeing the decoration of the Friends of Music tree, which glittered with little golden trumpets and treble clef ornaments. The whole place was bustling as people whipped their trees into shape. Smitty and Sam's uncle Dave, who worked for the hydro company, were stringing out extension cords and power bars for the lights.

Sam slipped the digital recorder from his pocket and pressed RECORD. Laughter echoed, ladders clattered, paper rustled. Down near the front, something shattered and voices groaned. Steve burped. On one side of them, Robert and some music nerds practiced harmonies as they put tinsel on a tree from their choir. On the other, Sam caught the whiskey-and-tobacco chuckle of Mrs. Goodenough as she helped with a tree from the Hope Springs Players. She saw Sam and waved.

"Hi," he called back, momentarily forgetting the recorder. "Hey, guess what? We have to read one of Mr. Goodenough's books for English."

"Really. Which one?"

"Um . . ." Sam realized he didn't have a clue. All he could recall was that the tattered paperback had the kind of prehistoric cover you saw on the ten-cent table at the Swap Shop. The book had been buried in his backpack ever since.

"It's *Dutch Courage.*" Amanda came to his rescue. Sam was grateful. How did she know that? She wasn't even in his English class.

She nudged him in the ribs and grinned. "Haven't you *read* it yet?"

"Oh lord," groaned Mrs. Goodenough. "Good luck. I don't think I finished that one myself."

"Now, I'm sure it's perfectly fine." Sam found Mrs. Doberman had somehow materialized among them, her smile locked in place. How had she done that? "Maybe I'll read it myself. Now, Dot, can I steal you away a minute?" She drew Mrs. Goodenough off, pointing out something about the trees.

Sam tucked away the recorder.

"How did you know that?" he asked Amanda.

"Delft told me."

"What for?"

"We're friends. She tells me lots of things. Girls talk, Sam."

Darryl, on the ladder, began talking also, explaining the best way to decorate the tree. They'd decided to use nothing but lights and foods from the Bin, in red and white. Everyone began stringing up candy canes, popcorn balls, foil-wrapped hearts, papaya spears and colored pastas. Still, the tree didn't look festive enough. Sam remembered the aluminum cookie cutters that his mom sold for Christmas baking. Delft suggested red bows from the flower shop. Darryl offered to go with her.

"Dream on, Darryl," Amanda said. "There's enough for us to do here. You'd get back next week. Hurry up, you guys"—she turned to Sam and Delft—"I've only got an hour." Off they went.

After the mustiness of the theater, the December air was bracing. They stopped at the Lint Lane mailbox while Delft deposited an airmail envelope. Carols arranged for syrupy classical strings wafted above them. Somehow, the music made him want to be in a band again, perhaps just to drown it out.

"That stuff is driving me crazy," he gestured to the speakers. "My mom has classical on in the store all the time, too."

Delft nodded. A sufferer of a variant malady, she said, turning in at the door of Hoog's Blooms, "Well, it's better than country."

Sam jogged on to the Bulging Bin, where he explained to his mom, then snatched up cookie cutters shaped like stars and moons and Christmas trees and stockings, as well as a grape bubblegum for personal consumption. Then, chewing, he grabbed a few more to share out back at the tree.

He scooted back through the Christmas strings to the flower shop, where he peered through the window for Delft. Mr. Hoogstratten was working today, he knew, and he still wasn't sure what his reception would be like. Delft's dad, however, cheerily waved him in.

"Stan!" he called, as Sam, deflating his gum bubble, stepped tentatively across the threshold. The door chimes sounded. "No need to stand out in the cold. Delft will be just a minute." The store was warmer than ever, and overflowing with poinsettias. Sam once again began to sweat. Country music burbled softly amongst the leaves as two clerks served other customers. In the midst of it all, Mr. Hoogstratten was expertly twining together a cedar wreath.

"So, how is your mom, Shirley?" he asked. "I'm glad we got all that kid stuff straightened out. I knew she'd see the light. Good for you, helping change her mind. I like a boy helps out. Here, hold this wire for a second."

Still pondering which, if any, of Mr. Hoogstratten's misapprehensions to correct, Sam took the wire. This, he'd suddenly realized, was his chance to ask about Madison Dakota. His hand trembled, causing the wire to bob up and down. Delft's dad fixed him with a look over his half-glasses. Sam sweated harder. "Say, you don't know a boy name of Darren, do you?"

"Darryl?" Sam croaked. His mouth had gone dry, despite his gum.

"That's him." Hoog Hoogstratten gave the wire a ferocious snip with the cutters. "There's a boy needs a job. Too much time on his hands for talk, talk, talk."

"His grandpa owns Handy Hardware," Sam said. "He said Darryl will be old enough to work there next summer."

"Won't be soon enough."

A voice more masculine than a dry shave began crooning over the sound system, *"A country tune, a pickup truck, and you—ou . . ."*

Mr. Hoogstratten hummed cheerily along. Sam realized it was now or never. "Last time I was in," he said quickly, wanting to get over that part, "I really liked the CD you were playing." He was still clutching the wire, as if it might pull him higher in Mr. Hoogstratten's estimation.

"Yah? You like country?"

"Oh, sure," Sam lied, clutching tighter.

"Which one was it?"

"Well," Sam said, taking the plunge. "I'm pretty sure it was Madison Dakota?"

"Madison Dakota!" thundered Mr. Hoogstratten.

Sam jumped. The wire clattered to the floor. "Yeah," he faltered. "In fact, I think she's from around here somewhere."

Storm clouds were brewing around Mr. Hoogstratten. His Abe Lincoln beard twitched ominously. "Is this some kind of joke?"

"What? No!" Sam babbled. "It's just, like, I saw her at the talent show, and I really liked her singing and I play music too and then I heard . . . and I just . . ." (This was true, and better than saying, "Well, she's this incredible babe, and I'd really like to . . .")

In either case, he had come to the limits of what he could articulate. Somehow he'd blown it again. He stood there sweating as Delft emerged from the back room, carrying a plastic bag full of red bows.

"Hi," she said. "All set?"

"Delft," Mr. Hoogstratten intoned. "Stan here likes Madison Dakota music."

"Oh?" she said, marching for the door. "Who's she? Well, we should go or we'll be late." She too must have been hot, because her face was red. "C'mon, Sam." The door chimed as she went out.

Sam turned to follow, but Mr. Hoogstratten said, "Wait. You really like her music?"

"I really like her singing." Sam tried to keep things truthful without causing an upset.

"What kind of music do you play?"

"Well, rock," admitted Sam, chewing his gum hard. Mr. Hoogstratten frowned. He added quickly, "But that's all you can get anybody to play. I like all kinds of stuff." Except country, he thought. And classical. And easy-listening. And show tunes. And folksingers. And opera. And jazz. And Christmas music. This seemed to be Sam's day for telling whoppers. He wondered if his nose was beginning to grow. But no, wait—he kind of liked his dad's Thelonius Monk CD. And the movie theme songs they played in school band. There: how well-rounded could you get? And the lying was for a good cause, *Lost* at the very least.

"Yah," said Mr. Hoogstratten, softening unexpectedly. "That's okay. You got to keep an open mind. Before I got into country, know what I liked, when I was a teenager? Soul. Otis Redding, Wilson Pickett, Sam Cooke, Jackie Wilson. Man, was I a greaser."

Sam briefly pondered who these people were and what a greaser might be as Mr. Hoogstratten reached under the counter. "Anyway, you're a good boy, Stan, and as long as it's just for the music, here."

He handed Sam a plastic-wrapped CD case. MADISON DAKOTA, it read over a picture of a white cowboy hat hanging from the side mirror of an old pickup truck. On the back, with the song titles, was a sunlit photo of a girl, smiling as she leaned against a rail fence in a meadow somewhere. Sam was startled to see that despite the jeans and boots and curls, she looked about eleven years old. Clearly this was not a new recording. Also clear was that despite the age difference and Sam's vagueness about the current Madison Dakota's face, she looked familiar.

"Oh wow," Sam said, "Thanks."

"Just keep it between us. Don't tell anybody, especially Delft," Mr. Hoogstratten said. "She doesn't like it."

"Sure, okay." In his relief Sam would have agreed to just about anything. He stuffed the CD into his jacket pocket and began to back up. "Thanks again. I'd better go."

"Open ears, open mind," said Mr. Hoogstratten. "Hey! Watch the poinsettias."

Sam stopped himself an instant before annihilating a display. He made amends by picking up the wire and passing it back to Mr. Hoogstratten, who said, "Who are you decorating this tree for?"

"The food bank."

"Those bums. You know, a lot that use that could get themselves jobs."

"Thanks, Mr. Hoogstratten." Sam slipped through the greenery and out the door before he could hear any more.

Delft was waiting impatiently outside.

"What took you?" she said, stamping in the cold.

"Um, your dad was saying something about the food bank."

"Oh." Her brow cleared beneath the stylishly silly ear-flapped hat she wore. As it did, the waning winter sun shone out from behind a passing cloud, bathing her face in a glow something like sunshine in a summer meadow.

"Oh, my God," Sam said. "You're Madison Dakota."

Chapter 15

D elft's face crumpled. "He *told* you!" she cried.

"Huh? No!" Sam protested. "Your dad didn't say anything. He gave me this CD and I recognized—" He began to tug the disc case from his pocket.

"No! Put it away! I hate that thing."

"But why?" Sam was bewildered.

"Why?" Delft shrieked. "Look at it!" Reversing her orders, she gestured for Sam to take out the CD. "See? It's so stupid. It's all country and I'm like this little kid with that dumb wig and the boots and makeup. Oh God, put it away!"

Sam obliged. Delft's eyes were wide. "Look, just don't tell anybody, okay? Please? It was my dad's idea, and it was fun maybe when I was ten or eleven and we used to go to all these country music things, but I don't want to do it anymore. The fall fair was my last Madison. He promised."

"But you're a great singer," Sam said.

"So what? I'm not Madison Dakota."

"Don't you like country music?"

"Sam, my dad likes country music. I already told you that. I just like singing. But not that way. Not anymore. Can you imagine how I'd get teased if everybody at school knew? Even just the wig— I mean, it was like you going around with that helmet on."

Sam cringed. "You still remember that?"

"Oh," Delft recovered herself. "Just barely. I mean, don't worry. Nobody thought it was your fault. It was sweet the way you put up with it."

"Oh," said Sam. "Wow. All this time I've been wondering about Madison Dakota—"

"That was sweet, too," said Delft. "Just please, please, please don't tell, okay?"

How could he refuse? Looking into Delft's eyes between her multicolored earflaps, Sam was staggered by the realization that in her own conservative non-Madison way, Delft was a *babe*. With a secret he now shared. Who sang. And whose parents had made her stand out by doing adult stuff when she didn't want to. They were soul mates.

"No problem," Sam said.

"Oh thanks, Sam." Delft gave a heartfelt sigh. She smiled. "I knew I could count on you."

Sam's heart made a small detour down to his stomach and back. Before he could speak, Delft said, "C'mon. We've got to finish the tree." She began to jog back to the theater. Sam followed. As they reached the doors, he thought to puff, "Hey, Delft? Is there other stuff you *would* sing? Not ADHD stuff," he hastened to add. "We broke up."

Delft's brow cleared again at this last statement. "You mean with you? Oh sure," she smiled. Opening the door, Sam pondered something else: Darryl was not going to like this. Oh, well. He blew a large, grape bubble as he savored the thought.

Back in the auditorium, many of the trees were ready. Steve was drinking a pop, clearly getting ready to rip out a few burps to test the acoustics. Amanda was talking with Robert and his friends. Ashley was on the stepladder. Larry was holding it. Darryl was pacing. "What took you guys?" he groused.

"I was talking to Delft's dad," Sam dropped what he thought was a provocative hint about changing times. Darryl, naturally, didn't get it.

"Well, let's get finished. They want to plug all the tree lights in at once." Darryl gestured over toward Smitty, who stood talking with Mrs. Doberman and Uncle Dave.

They finished stringing on the bows and cookie shapes as Mrs. Doberman called everybody to order.

"All right now. Just for fun, we're going to bring the houselights down a bit"— Uncle Dave waved from the back doors as he prepared to oblige—"and then we'll light all the trees at once, for a little bit of Christmas magic."

Everyone huddled a little closer, Sam and his friends clustered with Mrs. Goodenough, the Players, Robert, and his choir. Uncle Dave dimmed the lights. Smitty stood by another switch, below which was an outlet into which was plugged an industrial-size power bar. "Now!" cried Mrs. Doberman. Smitty threw the switch. All over the auditorium pinpoints of light flickered on. A collective "AAAAHHHH," filled the air, followed by a loud crackling and an even louder *FFFFTTTTTTTTTT* as the circuit blew, plunging the place into darkness.

A groan went up, then Sam heard shuffling in the blackness. Hands grabbed his arms, teeth collided with his, and he found himself on the receiving end of a poorly aimed but passionate kiss. He almost swallowed his gum.

"Hang on," Uncle Dave called, as an alarm began to clang. "The circuit's blown."

The hands let go. An instant later the houselights came back on. Uncle Dave ordered everyone outside, just in case. Everyone talked at once as they made their way to the doors. Except for Sam. Reeling, he looked at Delft. She looked back and smiled her shy Delft smile. It was enough: he knew. The *passion* behind that quiet exterior. How long had she felt this way? He looked to Darryl, jostling to step in behind her. Oh man, he thought, he really was going to have to break it to him. He looked to Amanda, who was staring at him, no doubt because of the blissful grin he felt on his face. Oh man, he was going to have to break it to *her*, too.

By the time they got outside, the first of the volunteer fire department had arrived, Mr. Gernsbach among them. They stumped back into the building with Smitty and Uncle Dave. A few minutes later they emerged, declaring everything safe. Mr. Gernsbach nodded to Sam as he went by, undoing the top of his fireproof coveralls.

"Sam the Man. No more Stomping these days. Your dad still cool with that?"

"I guess," Sam said, still savoring his first real smooch. "He said he needed a change."

"I think we all did. A change is as good as a rest, man." Mr. Gernsbach shrugged. Something glinted around his neck. "Well, keep on rockin'."

Sam nodded. It wasn't until later that the glint registered. Had it really been a string of pearls?

Chapter 16

"Too bad about Dad, huh?" Robin, newly home for the holidays, poked a thumb at their father's most recent copy of *Rolling Stone.* Mr. Foster's reading habits had changed of late, along with his appearance. Robin's own taste now ran more to the *New Yorker,* which Sam enjoyed for the cartoons. "He wants to borrow some of my CDs again, too. God. You know, some of that stuff is just not for them to listen to. I mean, old people could have a heart attack and die, or something."

Sam nodded and gently repositioned the tape recorder behind the poinsettia from Hoog's Blooms that currently graced the coffee table. He hadn't yet told Robin he was taping her, on the off-chance she might say something she might regret later. Blackmail was a survival skill he'd learned from his big sister.

"Like, not that Dad is totally old, not J. Earl Goodenough old," Robin fine-tuned her pronouncement as she slumped on the couch and picked up the magazine. "But really. I mean, come on: a *beard?* And it's gray, for God's sake. I nearly died when I got off the train. What does Mom say?"

Sam shrugged to indicate "nothing" and tried not to look at the recorder.

Robin sighed and flipped some pages. "I tried to be kind: I told him it would hide the necklace. But I'm telling you, Sam, I'm glad I'm out of here. I saw this in a movie: we're talking major midlife crisis."

Sam didn't take this too seriously, even though his dad had been adding to his new look in the ways she'd described. For one thing, he knew that Robin's track record for predictions was spotty. (She had once declared she'd be dead by seventeen, saying she intended to live fast, die young, and leave a good-looking corpse. Sam, naturally, had asked why she'd be better-looking dead than alive. He had then had to lock himself in the bathroom until their parents came home.) For another, he wasn't sure what a midlife crisis was, except that on TV it seemed to involve buying sports cars. That was something he figured he could live with, seeing as how he'd soon be old enough to drive. In the meantime, he deftly palmed the recorder as Robin bent over the magazine.

He strolled toward the family room door.

"Oh my God," said Robin behind him. "Has Dad seen this? There's an article about rock *guys* who may have had implants."

"What? Where?" asked Sam, meaning where was the article.

"Never mind," snapped Robin, misunderstanding. She didn't look up from the page.

Sam took the suggestion. With exams just over and the end-of-term dance on tonight, he had enough on his mind already. Romance was in the air, and proving to be as complex as the snowflakes that were swirling as well. Delft would be there. Amanda would be there. Unfortunately, so would his dad, as a staff supervisor. And Darryl. Sam hadn't quite gotten around to explaining how things stood to Darryl. Or to Amanda. Being a love god was trickier than he had thought it would be.

Sam was hoping that when Darryl saw Delft's preference for dancing with Sam, particularly on slow tunes, the Great Explainer would take the hint and realize that a better man had won. On the other hand, when Amanda saw Delft's preference for dancing with Sam, what would she think? Sam didn't want to hurt her feelings. Maybe she'd fall in love with someone else at the dance. But what if she didn't? On the other hand, it struck him as he walked down the hall, Amanda had said girls talked. Surely Delft would have told her by now about her budding romance with Sam. They were still friends, as far as Sam could see, so maybe everything was all right.

Temporarily relieved of this problem, Sam turned to another he'd been putting off: he didn't know how to dance. He went to his room to attempt to practice.

The darkened gym wasn't packed, but there was a respectable crowd by the time Sam and the others arrived. Music was ricocheting off the walls and up into the rafters. Colored lights flashed. Images gyrated on a video screen by the wall, next to the HAUL 'EM HUSKIES mural. Kids clustered along the walls, miming yelling and laughter. Or maybe they really were yelling and laughing; the music was too loud to tell. Every so often a group of girls—always girls—would scurry out and dance. Sam slipped out the recorder, muttered "High school dance," into it, then caught sounds until Steve burped. He had enough of Steve's burps on tape already.

A new video started up. "YESS!" Amanda, Ashley, and Delft dashed out and began dancing. Expertly. The boys looked at one another.

"Gonna dance?" Sam asked, praying the answer would be no.

Steve burped. Larry was looking around, clearly pretending not to hear. Darryl swallowed and said, "Yup." Then he ran after the girls, yelling, "Wait for meeeeee!"

Sam swore silently and looked over to the girls. They were bouncing and waving as Darryl caught up. It was now or never. All you had to do was jump up and down, right? Unless it was a slow dance, and then you had to . . . well, never mind that now. Taking a deep breath, he walked out to join the dancers. How hard could it be?

It was hard. The girls began enthusiastically demonstrating the moves he and Darryl needed to join in. Sam tried, feeling like a spastic pretzel. Darryl simply fell to the floor and cried, "Look! Break dancing!" Sam shuffled grimly as Darryl spun on his back, getting in everybody's way. At least trying to dance, instead of acting like a doofus, was going to mark him out to Delft as the most sensitive, in-touch, totally cool, who-cares-what-other-people-think grade nine guy around. Also, dancing with all three girls avoided the problem of exactly who he was really dancing with, just in case Delft hadn't had that heart-to-heart with Amanda yet. Finally, Sam figured, the gym was dark enough that no one else would notice.

He was midway through his third gyration, involving a foot drag into an embarrassing butt-twitch, finger wag, hands-to-opposite-shoulders move that Sam performed with the grace of a dead tree in a hurricane, when his dad strolled by. The lights seemed to glint off the silver in Mr. Foster's new beard as he bobbed his head in time to the music. Without looking at Sam he shot him two fingers, the gunslinger's salute, and strolled on. Sam, one finger in the air, felt himself blush from his boxers to the crown of his head. Too late, he dropped into Survival Slouch. Fortunately the song was ending. "I think I'll get a pop," he said.

The other guys were horsing around in the bleachers.

"Did you dance?" Larry asked.

Sam shrugged. He wasn't admitting to anything. All he could think now was if his dad blabbed to Robin, she'd be on his case until she went back to school in January. Why had his dad had to come by then? Shouldn't he have been off buying a sports car or something?

The girls came up, excited and red-faced, with Darryl right behind.

"Way to go, Sam!" from Amanda.

"It was easy, right?" from Delft.

"You should have seen me break dancing. It was soooo funny," from Darryl.

They all went out to the pop machine, where they got drinks and waited for Steve's obligatory burp. Then Darryl suggested, "Hey, wanta go to our lockers? I left my CD player there."

"We can't," Ashley said. "It's not allowed." Students were supposed to be only in supervised portions of the school.

"Come on," Darryl said. "What could happen? Is Sam's dad gonna expel us?"

Everyone looked at Sam. Sam didn't really want to sneak around the school. On the other hand, he didn't want to dance, or hang around near his dad, either. Besides, Darryl was just trying to look daring. If Sam refused, he'd look like a wuss. He looked at Darryl. "Maybe just you," he said. "Let's go."

Steve had become involved in a burping contest, but the rest hurried, giggling, along the hall, slipped past a caretaker's cart at an open classroom door, then ducked around the corner to the stairs. They ran up, passing a pair of skids necking on the landing and burst into the upstairs hall, giggling harder than ever.

"Hubba hubba," said Larry.

"Hickey heaven," said Ashley. Amanda, Delft, Sam, and Darryl smirked nervously.

The hallway was deserted. Everyone spoke in whispers as they moved through the eerie stillness, listening to their own footsteps. Afterward, Sam was never quite sure how it happened, except that Larry and Ashley stopped at the drinking fountain, then never did catch up, and that when they got to Sam's locker, Darryl somehow got them taking turns trying to fit inside and close the door. This involved just enough stuffing-in assistance to be exciting without being crude. Sam, of course, was the toughest fit, but he made it. No sooner had he crammed into the hopelessly narrow space than the door closed and he heard Darryl say, "Hey Delft, come on with me and we'll get my CD player."

Sam straightened up so fast that his head slammed into the locker shelf.

"Ow!" He tried to raise his hand to rub the bumped spot but found there was no room for that, either. "Amanda," he called, jiggling at the locker door, "Amanda! Let me out."

There was no answer. For a few seconds Sam listened to his own breathing. Then Amanda's voice whispered through the air vents. "Sam."

In the coffin-like darkness the intimacy of the sound was shocking. Sam bumped his head again.

"Ow! Let me out, okay?"

"Okay."

Sam waited, but the door didn't open. Instead, he heard Amanda whisper, "When the lights went out at the theater? It was really nice when you kissed me."

"What?" Sam was dumbfounded. "I didn't kiss you. Delft kissed *me.*"

"What are you talking about? She did not."

"She did too. She grabbed me and kissed me as soon as the lights went out."

"No! You grabbed my wrists and kissed me."

"No, I didn't! She grabbed me."

"Yeah, right," Amanda's tone hardened. "What was it, Trick Amanda Day or something? Who did it? Did you guys dare each other?"

"No! I—"

"Pretty funny, huh? I thought you didn't look at me after because you were too shy, but I guess you were trying not to laugh. Well, see how funny this is, bozo."

Through the door Sam heard the all-too-familiar rasp and click of his combination lock closing.

"No! Wait! Amanda!" he called over the retreating squelch of her sneakers. It was no use.

He pounded on the door and yelled some more. It occurred to him that it might be quite a while until anybody came this way, especially if the caretaker had already cleaned this floor. Classes were over until January. Had anybody seen them come up here? Surely Amanda would come back for him. Wouldn't she? His back was beginning to hurt. He pounded some more, then listened. No sneaker squeaks from the hallway. He had a panicky vision of Christmas in a locker. What if nobody came by until the New Year? Or years from now some shiny-faced niner would be assigned this locker and they'd have to cut it open and there would be his skeleton, still hunched, with a long white beard and hair to its knees . . .

"*Hellllp!*"

Darryl freed him a few minutes later. Sam was so relieved and so stooped that it took him a while to look high enough to see Darryl was alone.

"What happened?" Sam demanded. "Where did you go? I could have died in there!"

Darryl was too distracted to take in Sam's distress. "I don't get it," he kept repeating. "I just don't get it."

"Get what?" Sam grumped, rubbing his back. "You took off with Delft."

Darryl sighed and offered Sam a piece of bubblegum, the way he used to. "Yeah. Okay, I guess I better tell you: I kissed Delft."

"You *what?*" Sam straightened up. "While I was stuck in a locker?"

"No, no! That's the problem. It was at the theater, when we decorated the Christmas tree. Remember when the lights went out? Well, I grabbed her and kissed her. I guess I shouldn't have, but I just went for it. And now, when we go down to my locker, I try again and she gets all mad. So I say, well, I kissed you at the theater, and she says I never did."

Of course not, Sam thought, that's because she was kissing me. And then a light switched on. "Darryl," he laughed, unwrapping the gum. "You doofus. You didn't kiss Delft, you kissed Amanda by mistake. She just told me she thought I kissed her." Modesty forbade mentioning his own smooch with Delft. He began to chew instead. Grape.

"Huh?"

"Yeah. She said somebody grabbed her wrists and kissed her."

"Well, that wasn't me," Darryl said. "I grabbed Delft up near the shoulders. I swear to God. She was chewing grape gum like this."

Sam stopped rubbing his back. Another light was flickering to life. This one had a purplish glow.

"Oh man, Darryl," he said disgustedly. "That wasn't even Amanda. That was me."

Darryl's eyes bulged out and his lips retreated. "You! You didn't tell me you—"

"Why would I? I thought Delft kissed me."

"What would she want to kiss you for?"

Before Sam could answer, a voice called, "Hey, you guys, you're not supposed to be here."

They started, and saw Sam's dad strolling toward them. "Why the long face? said the bartender to the horse." Mr. Foster chuckled at his joke. His own eyes were gleaming. "Well, here's something to cheer you up. You guys are out of a band, right? So I'm starting a new one and you're going to be in it. C'mon, I'll tell you as we go downstairs."

All at once, Christmas in a locker didn't seem like such a bad idea.

Chapter 17

"What kind of a band?" asked Darryl as they walked down the stairs.

"Soul—rhythm and blues," enthused Mr. Foster. "A big, honking band that'll really cook: horns, rhythm section, backup singers, keys, the works. And of course"—he clapped the boys on the shoulders—"that rhythm section would need drums and a guitar."

"Oh yeah?" Darryl said, interested.

Sam cringed. Was this the crisis Robin had been gabbing about? He could imagine playing in an old-fart band with his dad. He *could* imagine it, but he didn't want to. The Stompers had certainly been better than ADHD—light-years better, in fact—but the music had been strictly from geezer land.

"I don't know if Darryl and I would fit in," he said. "You know, in a grownup band."

"Oh no, this won't just be grownups. Students, staff, and community members. Mr. Carnoostie and I are putting it together."

"You mean, it's for *school?*"

"Not exactly," Mr. Foster returned—a little testily, Sam thought. "I'd say it's more for fun."

"Well, who else is going to be in it?"

"Okay. We're looking at you guys on drums and guitar, Mr. Carnoostie on keyboards, Bob from the Stompers on sax, Amanda on sax and backing vocals, Vince from the Stompers on horn, me on vocals and horn, Robert Goodwood on trombone and backing vocals—"

"Larry on bass?" suggested Darryl.

"Actually, no. Just between us, I don't think Larry is quite ready for this. For that matter, you two will have to do a lot of practicing. Anyway, we're going with Carl Gernsbach on bass. You guys remember him, right?"

"Mr. Gernsbach plays the *banjo,*" Sam protested. Leaving aside the insinuation that Sam wasn't such a hot drummer, his dad had clearly gone off the rails. How could Sam be in a band with his own dad, a banjo-playing hippie, a nerdball water-walker who made music with snack food, and a girl who had just locked him in his own locker because he hadn't grabbed her in the dark?

"A tenor banjo," Mr. Foster corrected, pedantically. "He also drives a school bus, raises dogs, and volunteers with the fire department. But before any of that he was the bass player in a group called Buzzard Ugly, back in the sixties."

The name resonated with Sam, for reasons he couldn't begin to recall. For some reason Mr. Gernsbach's name also conjured up an image of a string of pearls. Life was too complicated.

"What kind of music did they play?" Darryl wanted to know.

"Oh wow." Mr. Foster puffed out his cheeks at the challenge of describing Buzzard Ugly's sound. "Sort of Captain Beefheart meets the Budapest String Quartet with a dash of, oh, the Supremes, you know?"

The boys looked at him blankly.

"Okay. Let's just say it was truly wild. The band also wore dresses."

"Even the guys?"

"It was *all* guys. A couple of them also had beards."

Sam thought again about pearls. Darryl said, "Hey, we're not gonna have to—"

"Of course not," said Mr. Foster. "That was a long time ago and something totally different. The point is, Mr. Gernsbach is an excellent bassist."

"Okay," said Sam, still protesting. "But Amanda? And Robert?"

"Hey," said Mr. Foster. "Mr. Carnoostie says Amanda is becoming a solid player. She reads well, sings well enough for backup, and she's got a good attitude. And Robert is an *excellent* musician. With that high voice he's got and all that harmony training for choir, he'll be perfect for backing vocals. He can help Amanda."

"But *you* singing?" Desperation was making Sam reckless.

Mr. Foster cleared his throat. "Hey, if anybody cared to notice, I've been singing in the shower for years. I'm a horn player, Sam— good breath control. And I've got that soul rasp when I need it."

"What if nobody wants to do it?" Sam played his last card.

"Oh, but they do." Mr. Foster smiled in satisfaction. "I called Vince and Bob, talked to Robert yesterday, and I talked to Amanda not five minutes ago. She joined so fast I didn't even get to mentioning you guys. In fact, the only thing we really need now is a female lead singer."

It took a downbeat for Sam to realize what his father had just said. When he did, he found he had also discovered something: his father's scheme was not boneheaded at all. It was positively brilliant.

"I know someone," he said.

"Who?" said his dad and Darryl.

"Never mind. I'll ask her." Who would have thought his dad could be this smart? It was a small Christmas miracle.

Chapter 18

Amanda and Delft, unsurprisingly, were gone from the dance, but Delft was delighted with the invitation to join when Sam called her the next morning. She made Sam reiterate his promise never to mention Madison Dakota. Then she said, "Amanda says you thought I kissed you."

Sam writhed on his end of the telephone. "Oh. Yeah. Sorry. That was, um, a mistake."

"Oh, don't be sorry. It was very sweet. You always think such sweet things. But it wasn't me. I . . . well, never mind."

"You what?" Sam persisted, still glowing from being called sweet.

"Oh, whatever. Who did kiss you?"

"Huh? Oh, it was a mistake."

"You mean someone didn't kiss you?"

"Well, kind of not exactly. Never mind."

Sam's next call was to Darryl.

"How did you even know she sings?" Darryl wondered.

"Geez," said Sam. "I thought everybody knew that. Don't you ever *talk* to her? And if you're gonna be in the band, I think you better call her and apologize."

Shortly afterward the phone rang for Mr. Foster. "The Hoogster's volunteered to help drive to gigs if we need it," he reported to Sam after hanging up. "He was kind of excited. I thought he was strictly a country guy, but apparently he's really into this music. He seems to like you, too."

"Cool," Sam said, and meant it. Both pieces of news were good. Delft wanted to join the band and had told her dad it was Sam's idea. Clearly, this meant that even if she hadn't kissed him madly in the dark it should not be ruled out on future occasions. He could definitely hear opportunity knocking.

Of course, there were two huge obstacles in the way of answering the door. Three, if you counted having to learn the music. The first obstacle was Amanda. When she found out on Saturday morning that Sam and Darryl were going to be in the band, she quit. This provoked a crisis, a sax player being essential to Mr. Foster's plan. "What is this all about?" Sam's dad wondered as he hung up the phone on her resignation call, a bare half-hour after Mr. Hoogstratten's.

"Probably she's just nervous," Sam had replied, nervous himself. There was no reason for adults to know the real reasons for things; it just confused them more. "I'll talk to her."

Sam had no idea what he was going to say to Amanda, but he wanted to say it right away. Now that Delft had joined, band harmony was a priority. He knew Amanda wasn't going to apologize to him about the locker, believing she'd been tricked. On the other hand, Sam figured he didn't have anything to apologize for either. He did, however, like Amanda (not kiss-in-the-dark like, but still . . .) and he felt badly for her. It wasn't her fault that he hadn't kissed her. In all modesty, he could see how she'd be disappointed that he hadn't. And he knew all about what it was like to be embarrassed. So, what to say? It was so far beyond him he had to take the ultimate risk: consulting Robin. He tried to leave out the more embarrassing bits.

Robin's inability to stop laughing when Sam described the band to her was the second obstacle. If this was a hint of things to come, there was going to be big trouble if they played anywhere.

"Robert Goodwood: soul man," Robin wheezed, weak from laughter. "Dad *singing*? God, I've gotta see this. You're in trouble,

Sam. It's times like this I wish Marlon was still around." Marlon was an ex-boyfriend who had carried his video camera everywhere. These days he attended a business college in Alberta.

"Oh yeah?" Sam scrambled to find a comeback and get Robin off-topic at the same time. Her opinion was too close to thoughts he'd already entertained himself. "Maybe we'll be good. At least I know music. You're the one who has to write a sports story for school and doesn't even know any sports."

"So? You have to write a book report about a J. Earl book and you don't know anything about it *or* writing."

"So? Maybe I'll get J. Earl to write it for me."

"So? Your band is still going to bite."

After these preliminaries had been cleared away, Robin did offer advice, for the steep but bearable price of doing some of her Christmas shopping and the semi-permanent loan of his Lizardlips CD. Sam listened, then went to Grandstand Sports and Collectibles to see Amanda. He took with him a copy of a CD his dad had burned with songs he'd downloaded for the band to learn. First rehearsal was set for the day after Boxing Day, not that far off.

The Grandstand was bustling with last-minute shoppers. Amanda, at the cash, gave no indication that she saw him. This was not a good sign. Sam selected a *SportsReports* magazine for Robin, half thinking it would be a good joke gift—there being nothing she'd be less interested in—and half thinking it might help with her sportswriting assignment. He joined the small lineup at the counter. Over in the hockey section he saw Robert Goodwood, apparently amusing himself with the different sounds he could get by clapping two pucks together.

Ahead of him, a grandfatherly type asked, "Would you have Snakes and Ladders?"

"Oh, no. You'd have to go to a pet store for that."

The man looked dumbfounded.

"Just kidding," Amanda said. "We don't carry board games, but they have it at the Hobby Shoppe."

When Sam's turn came, Amanda rang in the sale with no small talk whatsoever. "Five seventy-one."

Sam tried a smile while fishing out his duct-tape wallet. It stuck in his pocket. "I brought a CD of music we're going to learn. Everybody is hoping you'll come back."

"Just hurry up, okay? There's people behind you."

Sam gave the wallet a final tug and dislodged all the change in his pocket. Bending to pick it up, he bumped Ashley's mom behind him. Mrs. Trizzino in turn dropped an NHL sweater. Ashley had a thing for NHL sweaters. This one was for an expansion team no one liked. Ashley was going to be thrilled. Sam rose, red-faced, clutching wallet, change, and CD as Robert joined the line with his pucks. Amanda was rolling her eyes, but it was now or never.

"Listen," he blurted. "At the theater? It was not a joke, okay? Nobody was trying to trick you. I'm sorry you thought it was me who kissed you, but like I said, I thought Delft kissed me. But it wasn't—I was wrong, too."

Amanda colored. "Well, I told you that. She would have told me if she'd kissed you. And she wouldn't have kissed you anyway. Why would you even think that?"

"Why?" Sam was slightly offended. Geez. One second Amanda was mad because he hadn't kissed her and the next she was implying that nobody would want to smooch with him. At the same time, he knew he was walking a fine line here. "Listen, she has this secret, and I—"

"I *know* she has a secret. That's the whole point. I—"

Behind Sam, Mrs. Trizzino cleared her throat. Sam put the CD on the counter and dug out some money. Amanda began to make change. Sam tried again.

"Look, it was confusing, okay? I mean, Darryl got mixed up too. He thought—"

"I know what *he* thought. Delft told me."

"Well, there. See? All I mean is, you shouldn't be mad. You should be happy." It was time for Robin's advice. "Darryl didn't kiss you, right? And I didn't. So, if no one was tricking you, it means someone kissed you for real. Don't you get it? That means you have, like, a mystery admirer."

"Huh?" Amanda stopped what she was doing and stared at him. "Wow," she said, wonderingly.

"Maybe you should stop being mad and find out who it is."

"Wow," Amanda repeated, still in shock. Mrs. Trizzino cleared her throat again.

Amanda came to. She passed Sam his change and bagged the magazine and receipt. She smiled for the first time.

"So will you join up again?" Sam begged. He looked down the line to Robert. "She should join, right Robert?"

Robert, typically, blushed and nodded vigorously. Amanda rolled her eyes and smiled at him. Then she said to Sam, "So you must have a secret admirer too."

"Actually, no," Sam said.

"But somebody kissed you."

"Yeah, but I think I know who."

Mrs. Trizzino cleared her throat again.

"So who?"

"I'd rather not say."

As Mrs. Trizzino cleared her throat *again,* Amanda shrieked in delight.

"Ohmygod, Darryl kissed you!"

"Shhhh!" Sam pleaded. "You don't have to tell the whole world."

"Darryl kissed you?"

Sam grabbed his purchase and fled. Behind him, Amanda couldn't stop laughing.

"I'll join, I'll join!" reached his ears as he reached the door and escaped into the choral music wafting down the street from Lint Lane. What more could he do for love? Or art.

Chapter 19

As it turned out, there was another obstacle Sam had never dreamed of. It too related to the new band's image. Just before New Year's everyone gathered at Mr. Gernsbach's for their third practice. Sam, his dad, and Darryl rode out in Mr. Carnoostie's van, into which was also squeezed Sam's drums, Mr. Carnoostie's keyboard, Darryl's guitar and amp, Mr. Foster's horn case, a, briefcase stuffed with musical arrangements, and, nestled in Sam's pocket, O. Sidney Glebe's tape recorder. Mr. Carnoostie himself was squeezed into a winter coat and a flame-red tuque with a pompom, which in combination made him look even more inflated than usual. He and Mr. Foster discussed staffroom politics up front, while Sam and Darryl compared notes in the back.

"Did you practice?"

"Yeah." Darryl sighed. "I mean, it's okay. For like, old music, you know? But there aren't any big guitar solos, so I'm thinking of getting a side project going. This might be too easy for me."

"What about on *My Girl?* You have the best part."

"That's just one song." Darryl offered breath mints and for some minutes continued his description of why the music was too easy. Then he changed topics. "You should have seen what Larry and I did last night. It was so wild . . ." He went on to relate some tiresome hijinks involving Slurpees from the variety store. "I was gonna call you," Darryl finished, "but I didn't." Thanks for nothing,

Sam thought. He stared out at the drab, snowless landscape and dwelt uncharitably on how Darryl had actually fumbled his parts at the last practice.

This was easier than thinking about how hard some of his own drum parts had turned out to be. To Sam, the music on the practice CD had at first sounded interesting, but tinny and old-fashioned—not to mention foot-draggingly slow. Now his opinion was changing. Trying to play along, the tempos had come to seem more natural. In fact, he needed all the time he could get for some of the fills. Then, when he'd heard a few bars of the music live for the first time—a raggedy bit of "Midnight Hour"—he'd suddenly grasped some of the possibilities that must have struck his dad. The sheer volume of a nine-piece band had pinned his ears back, for one thing. And the horns reminded him of ska and the Recycled Lepers. Maybe after they'd learned a couple of geezer songs he could suggest a couple of Lepers songs. That would be cool. He had to make sure to ask Delft, among other things, if she liked the Leps.

The Gernsbach place was out on County Road Nine, just past the Hope Haven trailer park. Drifts of brown, unraked leaves clouded the lawn. Set behind the house, a suburban-style brick bungalow, were the kennels where the Gernsbachs bred golden retrievers and the workshop that was going to be used as a rehearsal space. Mr. Gernsbach's school bus was parked outside.

As the van pulled up, Mr. Foster half-turned. "Um, listen. Things are going well, so this might be the time to tell you that Carl can be, well, a little eccentric at home. I mean, nothing major. Totally harmless—and not all the time. After a while we didn't even notice with the Stompers, but if you're not ready, it can throw you a little. Now, there may be nothing today, maybe never. But if there is, just roll with it, okay? I'll mention it to the others, too."

Before anything else could be said, another van, emblazoned *Hoog's Blooms,* pulled in behind them. Everyone began unloading instruments. Mr. Hoogstratten waved and drove off. Sam hefted his bass drum and headed for Amanda, Delft, and Robert. Robert, as Sam already knew, was a really good musician. He was also chatting to the girls with an ease Sam could only dream of. How could a gay/weird, water-walker, browner band nerd do it? Maybe it was something you learned in grade eleven no matter what you were. Sam hoped so.

As he approached, Robert greeted him: "Hi, Sam. I was just reminding Amanda *again* that we have to work on that score for O. Sidney Glebe."

Robert's unbroken voice was, to Sam's ear, mincingly high. Sam shrugged a "Whenever" as gruffly as possible. The "ever" squeaked anyway. Sam winced. He felt doubly bad because Robert had reminded them of undone homework. Sam had spent three and a half minutes fretting over that very thing last night, as he'd microwaved some popcorn. He'd even vowed to do some (homework, not popcorn) soon. In fact, as the microwave hummed he'd gone so far as to skim the back jacket copy for *Dutch Courage,* the J. Earl book they'd been assigned for English. It promised "an epic adventure of daring and intrigue." "Gripping," "zesty," and "rollicking" had also caught his eye. Since fretting, vowing, and skimming all counted as homework, Sam had called it a night right there. The popcorn had been ready, and he and Robin had had *Slime VII* to watch. Fussbudget Robert, of course, probably had his work all done.

Now, as they headed across the gravel drive to the workshop, Sam slipped in beside Delft, a tricky move if you were carrying a bass drum with attached tom and foot pedal. Robert was still babbling away to Amanda, about hockey pucks, no doubt, or the fine points of high harmony. Sam had rehearsed what he was going to say.

"Could you help me with something tomorrow?"

Delft considered. "Well, maybe. I was going to do some homework. What is it?"

Ignoring the dreaded H-word, Sam explained Glebe's request for sounds. "I've already done some taping, but I need to do some more. If two of us went, we'd hear more." And fall in love, he added silently.

Delft said, "Neat. Okay, when do you want to do it?"

"I dunno. Maybe like, eleven-thirty. Is that too early?"

"No, that's good."

So, she was an early riser. Sam hugged this nugget of personal info close. Except for Christmas Day, he hadn't risen before noon himself. For Delft, he would.

"Okay. I'll meet you at Lint Lane."

Sam turned from her and saw he was about to walk straight into Mr. Carnoostie. He pulled up just in time. Mr. Carnoostie and the others were clustered around the open doorway of the workshop. In it stood Mr. Gernsbach, with Whiskey, his golden retriever. Mr. Gernsbach wore an understated ensemble of low-heeled shoes, a knee-length plaid skirt, and an accenting pale blue twinset, topped with a simple string of pearls Sam had seen before. Except for the breed of dog with him, and the way the cardigan sleeves rode up past the tattoos on his burly forearms, Mr. Gernsbach looked vaguely like the Queen.

"Hey man," he shrugged. "You either dig it or you don't, but I figured I might as well be up front from the start. At my place, this is me."

Chapter 20

The last stroke of noon died away from the clock tower on top of town hall. Sam switched off the tape recorder, then pulled it and his freezing fingers back inside the sleeve of his jacket.

"So, where do you want to go next?"

"Let's do the river."

They made their way through the deserted park, passing the band shell and the outsized plywood manger scene that Smitty and the Yeswecans erected every year to mark the season. Delft, Sam felt, looked particularly enchanting. She was wearing her flapped hat again. Matching mittens dangled on a string from the sleeves of the form-fitting ski jacket she wore above equally snug corduroys.

Together at last, he sighed to himself. Sam was seeing things as differently as he'd been hearing them. How could he not have noticed this girl? It boggled the mind. But now, here they were: roaming the town, together, on a cool secret mission for a famous musician. No parents, no siblings, no friends tagging along, getting in the way of romance.

By quarter to one they had recorded the river, the clunk of the library book drop, a train crossing the viaduct, a nickel going into a parking meter, and Delft laughing. Sam had insisted on the last one.

"Next?"

"Someplace warm."

"Want to go to Jimmy's for a slice?"

They went through the vacant lot that Sam's mom had wanted to be a teen space, to John Street and Jimmy's Pizza. Jimmy's steamy front window was filled with skids filling their faces. "Let's go to Marvin's instead," Sam suggested. They turned and took a route that led to Lint Lane. The wind blew snatches of a *Brandenburg Concerto* past them as they rounded the corner and ducked into the warmth of Marvin's Family Restaurant, two doors down from the Bin and across the street from Hoog's Blooms.

Their sleeves brushed as they shed their jackets in one of the booths. Sam blushed—how intimate could you get? Mrs. Marvin took their order for hot chocolates and fries to share. As they looked around the lunchtime crowd, Sam wondered if this qualified as a date. If it did, it would be his first.

"So," said Delft.

"So," said Sam. Fortunately, he'd made a mental list of conversational topics in advance. Putting Glebe's recorder on the table, he started with the most obvious. "What should we do next?"

"How about in here?" Delft nodded to indicate the restaurant itself.

"Okay." Sam pushed the RECORD button and leaned in close. "Marvin's Family Restaurant," he said. "Lunchtime, after Christmas." Sounds crowded the room. They listened to the clink of cutlery, the babble of conversations, and the background twang of oldies radio. Jackets rustled, upholstered benches squeaked, laughter rippled from the lunch counter, a blender whirred, plates clattered, the swing door to the kitchen bumped open.

When Sam hit the STOP button, Delft said, "We should get the music in Lint Lane too."

Sam nodded absently, lost for a moment in the glory of her almost totally zit-free features. Mrs. Marvin disturbed his reverie by thumping their hot chocolates down on the table.

"What? Oh yeah, sure," Sam nodded. They sipped their chocolate and thought up a couple more places. The whipped cream left an impish froth on Delft's upper lip. Sam thought about kissing it off and blushed some more.

"So what did you think of practice yesterday?" he asked. The older couple behind Delft levered themselves out of their booth. A couple of skids replaced them.

"It was fun, but what was with Darryl?"

For a while, Darryl had insisted on practicing while lying on his back.

"Oh, he was just being Darryl. He gets like that sometimes." Already it seemed as if Delft had been one of the group forever, instead of just meeting everyone in September. "One time last year he stood up in class and started waving his arms around and yelling 'Pay attention to me! Pay attention to me!' "

"Oh my God. Was he joking?"

"Kind of. I'm not sure. Anyway, you were great yesterday." Sam had had enough of thinking about Darryl, especially around Delft. And she had been great. The vocalists had run through several tunes with just Mr. Carnoostie comping at the keyboard. Delft's rendition of "What Becomes of the Brokenhearted" had all but blown the doors off the workshop. Everyone had applauded.

Now it was Delft's turn to blush. It was a heart-stopping sight. Sam outlined his idea of using some Recycled Lepers tunes and they tried to think of other current music they knew with horn parts. As they did, Delft looked past Sam and put on a formal smile. Sam turned. Mr. Hoogstratten had come over from the flower shop for a take-out coffee. He waved back to both of them, then turned for the door.

"Sam," Delft said in a thrillingly confidential tone. "Don't say anything about Mr. Gernsbach to my dad, okay?"

"What, you mean about him dressing up like a woman?" He dropped his voice guiltily as their fries arrived. "No. Okay. I wasn't going to tell anybody. Even though it is pretty weird."

Mr. Foster had told them afterward to take the dressing-up as a compliment. He said it meant that Mr. Gernsbach was comfortable with everyone.

"But I thought you said everybody in his old band wore dresses," Sam had said.

"That was something different, to shock people, a long time ago. Hey, I know it's odd. But it's harmless, so don't talk about it to other people. You know what gossip is like in Hope Springs."

Now Delft nodded in agreement. She took some fries and reached for the ketchup. "It is weird. My dad might not let me if he knew. He's kind of conservative? But don't you think it's kind of funny, too? I mean, he doesn't look a whole lot like a woman. Did you see those tattoos?"

"I've seen women with tattoos," Sam said, teasingly. Delft was bringing out his sophisticated, witty side.

"Yeah, but not anchors. And not there."

"So where do girls get tattoos?" Oh baby, how provocative could you get? Sam took some fries to hide the pounding of his heart.

Delft laughed. "You know. Lots of places."

"Well," Sam said, a little relieved, "I kind of thought he looked like a woman. He had makeup on and everything. And, uh, did you notice, like, up top?"

"His hair?"

"No! Not that up top. Up top . . ." Sam wiggled his fingers at his chest. Mr. Gernsbach had seemed more voluptuous in his twinset than he had in his Grateful Dead sweatshirt the day before.

"Ohhhhhhhhhhhh!"

They both exploded in giggles.

"How do you think he does *that?*"

More giggles, with mouths full. Sam fought back a chunk of fry that threatened to make a detour up his nose.

"Balloons?"

Sam snorted. The fry went up his nose. He was laughing too hard to care.

"He'd better be careful with his bass strap or he'll play *pop* music!"

Uncontrolled hilarity. Delft slammed into the back of the bench seat, her hand over her mouth, shaking with laughter. Sam's feet splayed out, one smacking the wall and the other the table leg. He could see the skids staring at them. Sam didn't care; it couldn't get any better than this.

When she recovered, Delft said, "Okay, maybe you're right. But he's never going to look like a movie star." She drained the last of her chocolate.

"You do," Sam wanted to say, but he had his mouth full of fries. He chewed furiously. *Hurry! Say it, say it,* urged a voice inside. From somewhere else inside, another voice warned, *If you do, you'll look totally stupid.* He slowed for a fatal second. Which was all it took for Delft to put her mug down and change the subject.

"Anyway. I guess that was our last practice before school starts. Have you done homework? I've got to do some this aft for sure. What time is it?"

Sam swallowed hard. The moment was gone. "It's about a quarter past one."

"Oh, wow. We should go. I have to get started. Have you done the math?"

"I haven't finished it." Or started it. Delft being studious, he didn't want to sound too slack. "Have you read that book yet?"

"Dutch Courage? I started it and now I can't find it. I'm going to ask my dad because he wanted to see it. Maybe he's got it."

"Why would your dad want to see it? 'Cause it's about Holland, like?"

Delft shrugged. "He said something about Mrs. Doberman knowing it. She's always buying flowers from us. Does she really like J. Earl Goodenough or something?"

Sam shook his head. "They don't get along very well." He didn't mention the episode of the lawn statues.

"So why would she want my dad to read one of his books?"

Sam shrugged, uninterested. Adults moved in mysterious and often boring ways.

It was time to go. Sam scooped up O. Sidney Glebe's tape recorder. They scrooched out of the booth. As they pulled on their jackets, Delft reverted to an earlier topic. "Gosh, I hope Darryl doesn't blab anything about Mr. Gernsbach wearing dresses, with that big mouth of his."

"Me too," Sam agreed.

As they headed for the cash register, one of the skids behind them said, "Pop!"

Sam saw Delft turn and throw them a suspicious glance, but he was too busy digging money out of his pocket to think any more about it.

Chapter 21

By the first day of school, Sam had his math done and his questions for history. J. Earl's novel lay undisturbed in his backpack right up until the bell rang for Mrs. Goldenrod's English class. This gave Sam a nervous twinge, but he knew he wouldn't be the only one who hadn't read *Dutch Courage*. He wondered if Delft had gotten around to finishing it. He'd forgotten to ask her as they'd walked to class.

As it turned out, it didn't matter. The first thing Mrs. Goldenrod did was to order everyone to hand in the book. "We're not going to study it," she sniffed.

This prompted three groans and two outraged *Whaat?*s from the five students who had actually done their reading. "Why not?" one demanded.

"Because," Mrs. Goldenrod bit off the words, "someone in the community has protested to the school board about it. Until the matter is resolved, we will study this." With that, she handed out copies of *A Tale of Two Cities.*

"It's too long!" went up the cry.

"Just be thankful it's not *War and Peace,*" Mrs. Goldenrod replied.

By the next day, a brief article about the protest had appeared in the Hope Springs *Eternal.* By the next, there were two letters in the paper about it and the Fosters' phone was ringing with a call from J. Earl Goodenough.

"That you, Foster?" the great man's voice rasped over the line when Sam answered. "Is my driveway shoveled?"

"What?" said Sam, putting down his guitar. "No. Why?"

"Why not? Aren't I paying you to shovel my drive?"

"But, like—" Confused, Sam peered outside. The ground was bare. "Look out the window."

"Well, I'm not going to see any snow if I look out the window, am I?"

"Huh? Then why are you asking?"

"Because there's no snow here, is there?" J. Earl was beginning to sound a little exercised. "I'm talking about where you are."

"But your driveway isn't here, it's there."

"What are you talking about? My driveway isn't here. It's up there!"

Was J. Earl lying on the floor? Sam was confounded. "Well, but . . . your driveway isn't here. It's across town at your house, where you are. And I don't think it's snowed there, either."

"Dammit, Foster. I'm not in Hope Springs, I'm in Mexico! Don't you remember anything?"

"Oh, yeah," said Sam, not really answering the question. Now that he thought about it, J. Earl had told him something about going away, back before Christmas.

"And this call is costing me a fortune, so start paying attention. Now, you've heard about this book banning?"

"Well, it's not exactly a banning. It's like—"

"Don't confuse the issue. I've already had calls from the CBC, Canadian Press, and the *Globe.* I'll be up Friday night. I want you to get some things and meet me at the high school the next morning. Eleven o'clock. Get Smitty to come, and tell your sister, too; she'll get an in-depth interview. Colleges love free-speech stories." J. Earl cackled. For a man whose book was under protest, he didn't sound too upset. He made Sam read back the list of things he needed, then hung up the phone.

The hammer and six-inch nails were easy: Smitty had them and he even offered to drive Sam and Robin over in his pickup truck. Robin was a bit harder to convince, being way behind on her sports profile. In fact, she hadn't started.

"He's just going to pull some stupid stunt and then blather at me."

"So? Maybe he'll help you with your sports thing."

"God," said Robin. "Yes. Why didn't I think of that? He knows *everyone*. Thanks, Sammy. I'll be there."

"Good," said Sam. In spite of himself, he was finding that he missed Robin—just a little—now that she was back at school.

The hard part was finding the copies of *Dutch Courage* that J. Earl had demanded. The students' books had been handed back in, and since the controversy began, any other available copies had been snapped up at the library and local used bookstore.

"We even called a bookstore in Toronto," Sam reported to J. Earl when he called to check on details, "and they said they don't make it anymore."

"Well, what did you expect?" huffed J. Earl. "I wrote it in 1958. Even my books go out of print, you know."

"Don't you have one?"

"Of course I do. Somewhere. But I'm not sacrificing it for something like this. It's a valuable collector's item."

As it turned out, Smitty had a copy of the book; so did the Gernsbachs.

"Why didn't you ask me?" Smitty said, as they drove out to get it Thursday evening.

"I dunno," Sam shrugged. In truth, Smitty had never struck him as much of a reader, although now that he thought about it, there was often a paperback or two in Smitty's truck.

Mrs. Gernsbach, a cheery lady who was stouter than her husband, asked them in while she went to get the book. Sam had never been in the house before. He looked around curiously. The place seemed bland for a person of Mr. Gernsbach's inclinations. Whiskey the retriever padded over for a hello sniff, then settled on the floor. From the corner a harsh, high-pitched voice cried, "Want a walk, Whiskey? Want a walkies?"

The dog scrambled up eagerly.

"Down, Whiskey," called Mrs. Gernsbach, returning with *Dutch Courage.* "And that's enough out of you," she said into the living room.

Something squawked, and Sam saw a parrot he had never met before either. It was perched on the back of an easy chair.

"He teases that dog all the time," said Mrs. Gernsbach.

Sam and Smitty went back out to the truck.

"Interesting place," said Smitty. *You don't know the half of it,* thought Sam.

Back at his own house Smitty produced his copy of the novel, a tattered paperback, much like Sam's had been, though even more defaced with ballpoint graffiti. Opening the cover, Sam saw a Hope Springs High School stamp. "Hey," he said.

"Don't tell Mrs. Goldenrod," said Smitty, seriously. He, like almost every other Hope Springer in the last thirty years, had been in her grade nine English class. She was a teacher you never forgot, and who, apparently, never forgot you.

"Weren't you supposed to hand these back in?" Sam asked.

"Yeah," Smitty admitted, "but I really liked it, so I kind of kept mine and told her I lost it."

"Tch, tch," came from Ms. Broom, who sat at the kitchen table marking grade six math tests. Now that he and Delft were almost an item, Sam could barely remember being in love with her. Grade six seemed lifetimes ago.

"Geez," Smitty was protesting. "I paid for it."

"I should go," said Sam.

Friday night Sam missed J. Earl's phone call because he was out at the movies. Larry had suggested they all go to see *I Wish You Were Dead Again* to take their minds off report cards. This was mostly a joke; everyone but Darryl had done pretty well.

"How can you fail music?" Amanda had wrinkled her nose at Darryl as they walked home.

"I just never remember to hand stuff in," Darryl shrugged. "But Mr. Carnoostie said if I finish some of the old assignments and hand them in this term, he'd still give me credit. Raise my mark, like. Hey Sam, can I borrow your music notes this weekend?"

After supper, Sam took the notes to Darryl's. Larry's mom would pick the boys up there. The Sweeney house was still ablaze with Christmas lights, a given since Darryl's parents worked at his grandfather's hardware store. Sam liked it. On a good year at the Fosters', Sam's dad strung a lone strand of lights along the front porch railing. Then no one ever remembered to turn them on.

Inside, the house was bursting at the seams. Melissa and some of her teammates had stopped in on their way to a university volleyball tournament. They filled the kitchen, talking all at once, as Darryl's mom laughed with them and put out snacks. In the living room, Darryl's brother Ryan was reciting something to their dad, who held an open binder.

"He's got a lead part in *The Secret Garden*," Darryl explained. "They're practicing." He flipped open Sam's music folder. "Has it got—" His brow wrinkled, then he grinned. Sam felt a twinge of apprehension; what the heck was Darryl looking at? "Hey—oh yeah. Never mind." Darryl closed it and leaned into the living room, interrupting his brother. "Dad, Dad! Sam brought me his notes, so I promise I'll do it tomorrow, okay? Can I go now? Please?"

"Darryl, c'mon," Mr. Sweeney said. "We're trying to work here."

"Sorry. But can I go now? Please?"

For an instant, Sam meanly wished Mr. Sweeney would say no. It would serve Darryl right for all the times he'd tried to leave Sam out, and let Sam enjoy an evening that included Delft. Instead, Mr. Sweeney said, "Darryl, if those music assignments aren't on the kitchen table tomorrow when I get home from work, you're grounded. No band, no anything. Understand?"

"They'll be done, they'll be done, I promise. Just, can I go?"

Outside, a horn honked. Larry's mom had arrived with their drive. Mr. Sweeney nodded wearily. "Just remember what I said. Hi, Sam."

"Hi, Mr. Sweeney. Hi, Ryan." Darryl already had his coat on and the door open. Hats, gloves, and boots were formalities teens dispensed with, even in January. "Let's go," he said. "BYE."

Sam wasn't sure whether anyone heard or not.

Next morning was bright and cold. An inch or so of snow had fallen, just enough to leave the world rimed in a white glare that made Sam wish for sunglasses as he and Smitty and Robin huddled blearily in the extended cab of Smitty's pickup. They were waiting for J. Earl in the high school parking lot, which, as usual, was fairly crowded.

"So let me get this straight," Robin yawned, being an even-later riser than Sam on weekends. "The group is called FIDO?" She had a pen and open notebook on her lap.

"FIDOD," Smitty sipped from his oversized car coffee mug. "Finger In the Dike of Decency. They say the book is unfair to the Dutch."

"Unfair to the *Dutch?*" Robin made an unbelieving face as she wrote, or maybe she was just squinting. Sam was too tired to tell.

Smitty shrugged behind his wraparound ski shades. The gold pompom on his Boston Bruins tuque bobbed. "There's a lot of Dutch people came here after the war. Some of them are pretty conservative."

"So, this isn't even, like, a religious protest or witchcraft or too much sex?"

"Too much sex?" Sam perked up and reached for the shopping bag containing the two copies of the book.

"Nah," Smitty said. "They say it makes them look dumb and too scared of the Germans."

"Stereotyping," said Robin.

"But the title says they're brave," Sam offered.

"Not exactly." Smitty looked out the window. "It's an old British slang thing for booze—some people feel tougher if they're drunk. The Dutch make gin: courage in a bottle, get it? 'Course the English and the Dutch used to be enemies, so it's also like saying that if you're Dutch you're a chicken unless you've been drinking."

"So, who are some of these people?" Robin asked as she wrote. "I guess I'd better interview them, too."

"Well . . ." Smitty began. At that moment a station wagon Sam recognized pulled in beside them and out popped J. Earl Goodenough, resplendent in the biggest mitts and parka Sam had ever seen. Smitty put down his window. Sam slipped out the tape recorder and turned it on.

"All set?" boomed J. Earl. His breath bloomed in the cold.

"I guess," said Smitty. "What are we doing?"

"You'll see in a few minutes. There room for me in there?"

Smitty scrooched the seat forward and J. Earl bundled himself and the voluminous coat into the small back seat. He looked approvingly at the ranks of cars. "Good crowd," he nodded, then frowned. "But what do they all have to drive here for? When I was a boy, by God, you walked—"

"What are we waiting for, Mr. Goodenough?" Robin interrupted. Both she and Sam had heard this speech before. "Can we start the interview now?"

"Not yet," said J. Earl. "The camera crew oughta be here any minute."

"Camera crew?" said Sam.

"So much for an exclusive," Robin muttered, interrupting. "Can I ask you something else then?" She went on to explain her sportswriting assignment.

"Sure, I can suggest somebody I know," J. Earl nodded. "Francis Xavier Muldoon."

"Who?" said Sam.

"He was a goalie for the Leafs back in the thirties," Smitty filled in.

"Not *a* goalie," J. Earl huffed. "The best goalie they ever had! Xavier the Savior, the papers called him when I was a boy. We worshipped the ground he walked on. A Catholic hockey star in Protestant Toronto, back when nonsense like that mattered. There's your angle, in fact. And he was a helluva guy, to boot. I knew him well. He got a bunch of us started one way or another."

Robin looked impressed. "Could you introduce me?" she asked.

"Only at a séance," said J. Earl. "He died in 1962, choked on a communion wafer. I went to the funeral. But you'll find lots in the old Toronto papers—and, of course, you can interview me extensively. But not now, they're here. Come on."

A van with the Canadian Broadcasting Corporation logo on its side had pulled up before the front doors of the high school. J. Earl squeezed out of the truck and strode to greet them, his fur-lined hood bouncing behind the shiny dome of his head. Sam and the others followed with hammer, nails, and books.

The cameraman set up his tripod in front of the doors. J. Earl clipped a lapel microphone to his parka, and someone who seemed to be a reporter checked his hair in the side mirror of the van. The three of them conferred and then J. Earl waved Sam over. Sam slipped the tape recorder into his pocket and joined him.

"All right," said J. Earl. "You carry those, I carry the books. Ready? Let's go."

With the camera rolling, J. Earl marched toward the front doors of Hope Springs High.

"But what are we doing?" Sam called, hurrying to keep up.

"Ever hear of Martin Luther?" J. Earl's words clouded out over his shoulder.

"Wasn't he in *Cold Blood, Hot Lead?*"

"Never mind," J. Earl growled. They had reached the doors. "Here. Give me that stuff. Just hold the book up like that." He positioned a copy of *Dutch Courage* against the door. Being several inches taller than the great man, Sam held it easily, but warily. J. Earl lifted a six-inch nail and the hammer and proceeded to pound it into the book, trying to nail it to the door. The door banged and rattled alarmingly.

"Hey!" Sam was shocked—and also afraid for his fingers. "You can't do that, we'll get in trouble! The school—and that's Mr. Gernsbach's book!"

"Don't worry about it," J. Earl puffed as he pounded. "Trouble is the whole idea. With any luck, the whole school will be pouring out here in a minute to see what the racket is."

"No, they won't," said Sam.

"Why not? Are they deaf in there or something?" J. Earl kept on pounding. "God, this thing is thicker than I thought."

"They're not deaf. It's Saturday. No one's here."

"Saturday?" J. Earl paused in mid-swing. "Saturday? But then what are all the cars—"

"They park here to go to the arena next door. For minor hockey."

"Damn!" said J. Earl. "Why didn't you tell me?"

"But . . ." Sam protested. "You said Sat—"

"Never mind, I'll let it go. The bloody nail won't go in, either. Well, don't worry, we'll just have to make the best of it. Cut!" J. Earl called, turning to the camera. "Listen, have you got some duct tape or something we can use to stick this bloody book to the door?"

The filming took a while, and by the time it was done, Sam was freezing. J. Earl didn't seem to mind at all. A modest crowd of curious hockey commuters had gathered to watch. He joshed with them between shots.

"They can protest my work," he said finally into the camera with a steely glare and a determined voice, "but I protest them. You can't nail down free speech!" In one hand he shook the hammer. With the other he reached up and clapped Sam on the shoulder. "And as long as I have loyal, freethinking readers like this one, free speech and I will prevail!"

Chapter 22

1. "It was the best of times, it was the worst of times"
is an example of:
   (a) a metaphor
   (b) a paradox
   (c) personification
   (d) synecdoche
   Explain how something can be the best and worst at
   the same time. Offer an example from your own life
   experience.

Sam put his pen down on the kitchen table and scowled at the question sheet. Why did English homework always have to take so long? Behind him his dad clattered the roasting pan in the kitchen sink. Sam wished he could have some music on to take his mind off his work while he did it, but he wasn't allowed to. Anyway, he only had twenty-five minutes to get this done before it would be time to leave for music practice.

The best of times, the worst of times. Well, that was easy—how about right now? Best: he'd solved the mystery of Madison Dakota and was now in a band (and getting along wonderfully) with real-life babe Delft Hoogstratten. Worst: Darryl had found Sam's embarrassingly passionate Madison Dakota doodles on the inside of his music folder and was telling the world that Sam was drooling over a country singer in a cowboy hat. He made it sound as if Sam was gaga over a cartoon character, and Sam, having promised to keep Delft's secret, couldn't strike back by saying who Madison Dakota really was. Home with the flu, Delft hadn't even been there to watch him suffer for her.

Another best: he'd just been on the national news and he had the videotape to prove it. Worst: Everyone agreed that he'd looked like an idiot, especially in the part where he'd been asked for his own comments on *Dutch Courage*. He'd said it wasn't like all Dutch people were drunk chickens. Well, geeeeez, Sam thought. It wasn't his idea to be there; J. Earl had dragged him out. How could he say he hadn't read the book?

Come to think of it, it was kind of a best/worst for J. Earl, too. First he'd chuckled, "Don't let them kid you, Foster: no news is bad news. There's no such thing as bad publicity. This is just what the doctor ordered." Then he'd gotten quite grumpy when an innocent question from Robin revealed that Mrs. Goodenough was still down in Mexico and that one of their neighbors there was O. Sidney Glebe.

"Hey," Sam had blurted. Something had just struck him and he thought it might lighten the mood. "O. Sidney Glebe, J. Earl Goodenough. Your names have the same pattern."

"Don't even mention it," J. Earl had glowered.

"Better get cracking, Sam. We have to leave for music in twenty." His dad sat the upturned pan in the drainboard and walked by, wiping his hands on a tea towel. His ponytail was getting longer.

Sam sighed and picked up his pen. Music itself was another best/worst. The new band had a couple of songs more or less under its belt, and they were beginning to get the hang of some others. Compared to the speed at which ADHD had picked up tunes, this was mind-boggling progress. And for old-fart music, the tunes sounded good. Practice was fun; Delft was there, of course (except she wouldn't be tonight, given the flu), and Mr. Gernsbach always wore something interesting.

On the down side, a couple of grade eleven kids had asked him in the music room yesterday if he was really going to be in a band with "Foster and Carnoostie." Clearly his questioners weren't aware that "Foster" was his dad, a good thing. Bad was their follow-up question: Were they all going to grow ponytails like Foster or guts like Carnoostie? Sam sagged in his chair. Just wait till everyone found out about Robert being in there too. Or, God forbid, about Mr. Gernsbach's wardrobe. Didn't he have enough on his plate with the Madison Dakota thing? The teasing would never end; his Survival Slouch would be a permanent posture.

"Sam." Another warning from his dad.

"I'm thinking." You couldn't argue with that. He wrote the number one on his page and guessed *(b)* was the answer. Surely they weren't expected to look up definitions for all those things.

The phone rang. Mr. Foster answered, then said, "Elvira, hi! Uh-huh. Sure, he's right here." He passed the phone to Sam. "Speak of the devil."

"Huh?" Sam took the phone. What was this about? "Hello?"

"Hello, Sam. This is Mrs. Goldenrod."

"Oh." Mrs. Goldenrod was not among Sam's usual callers. "Uh, hi. I'm doing my English right now, so I don't forget," he said quickly, in case she was checking.

"Good," said Mrs. Goldenrod. "I'll be sure to call on you tomorrow." Sam groaned inwardly. "But that's not why I called. I saw you and Earl Goodenough on the news on the weekend and I want to congratulate you for taking a stand against censorship."

"Oh, uh, sure. Thanks."

"Not everybody has the courage to speak up for what they believe in. I was also pleasantly surprised to see you'd read the book."

"Yeah, well, that's okay." Sam found himself shrugging, although Mrs. Goldenrod couldn't see him. He also wasn't too sure just what was okay, but it sounded about right.

"It's better than okay. Now, Sam, I'm going to suggest something. I know now you're independent enough to make up your own mind. The school board is meeting to discuss this protest next week. I'd like you to go and speak to them, as a student. Tell them what you thought of the book. Show them that high school students are capable of thinking for themselves."

"Well . . ." Sam couldn't think of anything he wanted to do less, except maybe his math homework, and even that he'd get to be dumb at privately. The problem was, adults saying, "I know you can make up your own mind" when they asked you to do things was just a disguised way of saying, "Do it or die."

"Sam," Mrs. Goldenrod went on, "I've known Earl Goodenough almost since he moved to town in the sixties. He may not show it, but this hurts him: his own town saying one of his books isn't fit to be read. For all the noise he can make, he needs someone in his corner, too. Think about it."

Mrs. Goldenrod said goodbye and hung up. All at once the receiver seemed to weigh a thousand pounds. Sam hung up. The phone rang again. It was J. Earl Goodenough. Sam looked quickly out the window.

"It hasn't snowed any more. Your driveway is fine."

"I know that, Foster. I just parked in it."

"Oh. Didn't you go back to Mexico?"

"Obviously not. And I'm not going back until this book business is settled. Free speech, free publicity, the whole bit. That's why I'm calling. Did you see us on the news? We made a real team, there."

"I guess."

"Darn straight. Now listen. There's a school board meeting next week . . ."

Sam listened as J. Earl also made a pitch for him to take part. "It's supposed to be beneath my dignity, but I'm going to get up there and talk myself, which, if I may say, will guarantee us national media coverage, and I'll introduce you as my protégé—"

"Your what?"

"Never mind. The point is, you'll be an instant celebrity— the schoolboy champion of free speech—*and* we'll humiliate these yokels. It can't lead anywhere but up. Think it over. Let me know."

Sam hung up again. As he sat back down, he felt his spirits begin to soar. Forget the adult pressure, he'd just seen things in a new light. It wasn't just nationwide celebrity, Sam told himself. Mrs. Goldenrod was obviously right: J. Earl needed some help on this one. If he started ranting about yokels, well, imagine what would happen. Besides, Sam owed it to teens everywhere to show that kids could think for themselves. Even more important, being a poster boy against censorship might show one teen in particular what a cool guy he truly, truly was. So he'd do it. He'd even read the book. But he wouldn't tell J. Earl yet. First he was going to tell Delft, just casually. He wouldn't tell her about Darryl's teasing, though. She'd hear about that anyway, Darryl being Darryl. When she found out how he'd loyally kept her secret, and put that together with his modesty about being a celebrity, well, would she be impressed or what? And after he'd impressed her, he'd ask her on a date.

He lifted his pen and wrote *Good – being a celebritty.* Then he crossed out *celebrity* and substituted *well known* which sounded a bit more modest, and added *Bad – everybody wanting you to do stuff for them.*

Chapter 23

Unfortunately, Delft wasn't around to be asked for the next few days, still being home sick. Darryl and his teasing remained maddeningly healthy. Sam didn't bother to mention the school board to him. Sam's parents, however, had been impressed.

"Good for you," his dad said. "We're proud of you. Let your voice be heard."

"What are you going to say?" inquired his mom, who had more practical experience in dealing with boards and committees.

"I'm not sure yet. I'm working on it." This seemed a better answer than "I dunno. I have to read the book first."

"Well, if you want to talk it over with us," said Mr. Foster, "feel free, any time. I was looking at a copy at school yesterday. Haven't read it since I was your age."

Meanwhile, at school, Mr. Carnoostie reminded everyone that O. Sidney Glebe's return visit was the next day. Listening to the chorus of "You never told us!" the music teacher pointed to a notice on the blackboard that had indeed been there for months, giving the date the assignment was due. "The music room will be open after school, as always," he said.

Sam guessed this also meant Glebe would want to listen to his tapes, giving him one more thing to organize this evening. After school he met Robert and Amanda in the music room. Several other groups were already huddled, puzzling over Glebe's cryptic score. Sam was relieved to see Darryl's group was not among them.

They looked at the circular pattern of symbols. "Where should we start?" Sam asked.

"Anywhere," Robert lisped confidently. "A circle has no beginning or end."

Amanda nodded. "Okay. Let's end at the black dot. That's got to be a big heavy sound."

"So we start at the empty square. That'll be light and even: four equal sides."

"Like taps on a high hat," suggested Sam the drummer. He was beginning to get the idea.

Robert nodded and made a note on his page. "Four beats, four times."

They kept at it until Mr. Carnoostie said he had to lock up. It was then that Sam remembered they also needed a definition of music. He volunteered to look one up as Robert and Amanda continued to discuss orchestrating the spiral. They didn't hear him.

"I start stretching a rubber band and you pluck it faster and faster!"

"I said, 'I'll get a definition for music,' you guys." Sam hoped this would result in expressions of gratitude. What he got was Robert saying, "Okay, then we'll keep on with this. Meet back here before school tomorrow. We can get in at seven-fifteen to rehearse."

Seven-fifteen! That would mean getting up at six-thirty. Sam thought of math homework, *Dutch Courage,* organizing the tapes for Glebe, and various sitcom reruns that he had hoped would keep him up late. And this wasn't even for marks! He waited for Amanda to protest. She didn't, so he nodded reluctantly. Robert's suggestion made sense. Besides, he could always show up a little late. Geez, he was about to stand up for their rights and be a national hero.

Outside, it had snowed. Robert and Amanda went off, still debating sounds. Sam hoofed it home to drop off his books and then go to clear J. Earl's walk and driveway. Since the great man was home, he'd want it done right away. Sam wondered if he'd still have to do this after he stuck up for J. Earl at the school board.

At the moment, though, he didn't really mind. It felt good to be exercising in the twilit chill after the lights and oppressive warmth of the school. The Overloaded Circuits howled in his earphones until his shoveling made the CD skip. He paused to pull out the phones and felt air rush into his ears the way it had back at the fall fair. He listened to his shovel scrape on the asphalt. The powdery snow *whumped* lightly onto the freshly covered lawn. A streetlamp buzzed overhead. Somewhere nearby a car spun its wheels.

Lamps glowed inside the Goodenough house. After a while the front door opened. J. Earl stood framed behind the glass in the screen door. When Sam finished, he walked over. J. Earl had his money in one hand and a glass of something in the other. Music was playing in the background. J. Earl, however, wanted to talk about the school board meeting.

"I can't right now," Sam said. "I've got all this homework. I have to make a definition of music." At the moment he was glad of it, too. He didn't want J. Earl to learn he hadn't read his book yet, either.

"Definition of—you can't define music, Foster. It's different for everybody. It's all in the way you hear it. The best you can try to do is pin down the essence of each piece. I remember I once described a Dexter Gordon solo as 'maple syrup laced with nitro-glycerin.' Nice, huh?"

"Yeah," Sam agreed. He wondered who Dexter Gordon was. Clearly he was Canadian since he used maple syrup.

"I mean, to me, that's music. *This* is music." J. Earl jerked his chin back toward the sounds from his living room. Now that Sam was taller than J. Earl, he had a better appreciation of how the light played off the great man's head. "Listen," ordered J. Earl, pushing the door wider. "Just *listen* to that."

A breathy sax solo curled like wood smoke into the January air. "'In A Sentimental Mood,' Duke Ellington. That's Paul Gonsalves on tenor. That's it. That's music for me, the way I hear it. What's music for you"—he waved his glass at the earphone poking over the collar of Sam's jacket, sloshing out some of his drink—"God knows, except I won't like it.

"And then," he said, his brow darkening, "there's that crap Glebe calls music: plucking on fence wire and hitting pianos with hammers. Choirs doing random burping. You get more melody with a musical saw."

J. Earl was getting quite animated by now; the ice cubes were rattling in his glass. Clearly a rant was coming on. Sometimes these led to commentaries you saw later on TV. Now, however, was not a good time to listen. Sam excused himself and headed home to work, envying J. Earl's adult freedom to sit around and listen to music. On the way, he wondered if he could incorporate fence wire into his music answer, just to be safe.

Chapter 24

The performances the next day were different, to say the least. Sam, still a little groggy from his early rise, figured he and Amanda and Robert did as well as anyone else, and certainly better than Darryl's group, who did too much fumbling and giggling. All through first period sandpaper scraped, feet thumped, saxophones honked and swooped, pie plates rattled, elastics twanged, and, memorably, air was released from a balloon to create a spiral of sound that wound its way from a squeal down to guttural flatulence.

The maestro, as Mr. Carnoostie referred to him, sporting a Mexican tan and a bulky black fisherman's sweater that engulfed him to his silvery chin, sat attentively, head back, nose aloft, finger pointing to temple. His eyes closed as he listened. When the last performance was done he led a round of applause for everyone. "Well," said O. Sidney Glebe, "but is it music? In fact, what is music? What have you decided for me?"

Most of the comments that followed came straight from various dictionaries. Sam could tell, because that's where his had come from. Bulky phrases like "harmonious rhythmic patterns," "beauty of form," "satisfying expression of emotions," and "pleasing to hear" tumbled awkwardly about.

"So music is something expressive you make." Glebe paused. "Who makes it?"

"Musicians."

"What makes a musician?"

"Being able to play or sing. Like, if you can make musical sounds."

"Can anything besides people make music? Do birds? Babbling brooks?"

The group chewed this over for a while, except for the usual few, who had busy doodling schedules. For the others, it seemed to depend on how nice the sounds were. Glebe interrupted. "But why all this *nice* and *beauty* and *pleasing*? What if something sounds unpleasant? A car horn, is that music?"

"No."

"All right," Glebe said. "May I?" He plucked a CD case from a desk. *Chronic Death Jam.* I've heard this—my grandson has it. Music?"

"Sure."

"Sounds like car horns to me. Mozart: music?"

Groans, but heads nodded.

"Yet people use his sounds to drive kids away. Is it still music?"

"Well, obviously it's just everybody has different tastes," a girl said.

"Ah. Then who's to decide what's pleasing or not, what's music or not? Why can't a car horn be music? My friend John Cage used to say that music is sound. Does that mean everything is music?"

"It means it could be," said Robert, slowly.

"Could be, if what?"

"It's all in the—if that's the way you hear it," Sam blurted, immediately feeling embarrassed. The phrase had popped up, ready-made.

Glebe cocked his head at him. "Ah. So who else helps create music?"

"Listeners," said Robert.

"It's an interesting idea, I think: listening creatively. I've enjoyed working on it with you." He thrust back his chair and stood up. Apparently they were done.

Voices struck up all around. Mr. Carnoostie called something over the din. Glebe finished saying something to a student, smiled, then turned and beckoned to Sam. "I'd like to meet here after school to listen to some tape, if you don't mind."

Sam could recognize a polite order when he heard one. "Sure, I've got it here." In fact, the recorder was in his pants pocket. He'd used it to secretly tape the morning's performances. Now he popped in the earphone and hit REWIND, hoping to find the expiring balloon. The bell rang. As he walked out the door, he found himself listening to someone passing in the hall instead.

"Hey, Foster," the skid called. "Do you all wear dresses when you play music with that fag Gernsbach?"

Chapter 25

Sam had grown quite fond of taping sounds around Hope
Springs. He'd also kept track of his work so successfully, for a
forgetful guy in grade nine, that nearly half the sounds were identified.
And though he'd been looking forward to showing them off, he was
nervous as he played some of the tapes to O. Sidney Glebe while Mr.
Carnoostie pottered in the background. Partly, this was because the
taunt about Mr. Gernsbach had been ringing in his ears all day.
Partly it was because listening to the playback, the sounds on their
own seemed ridiculous. How could he have chosen this stuff?

Glebe, however, seemed to be enjoying himself. He had
hooked the tape machine to a small speaker that now sat beside it
on the desk. Glebe himself perched in his listening pose, smiling
faintly at various snippets of tape while Sam anxiously watched his
reaction. Then, unannounced, J. Earl's voice erupted from the
speaker. It was his conversation with Robin about Muldoon, the
hockey player. Sam cringed.

"That was a mistake. I, uh . . ."

Glebe, eyes closed, raised a finger to quiet Sam's protest.
When the segment was over he stopped the tape and looked away,
oddly distracted. Finally he said, "How interesting. Does Earl
know about this tape?"

Sam shook his head.

"He doesn't care for me, you know."

"I know. Once I said that your names had the same pattern and he got mad."

Glebe's eyebrows flickered. His mouth pursed in amusement. "Really? Well, I suggest you ask him sometime what the J. stands for. Say the Black Spot will get him if he doesn't tell."

"Sure," Sam said. He wouldn't, of course, but it was safer to humor old people.

"For example," Glebe continued, clearly savoring the nugget of information he was about to impart, "the O in my name stands for nothing."

Sam squinted. "I don't get it."

"Nothing," Glebe repeated triumphantly. "O equals zero equals nothing, and sometimes nothing can sound wonderful. It's very different from a black spot."

"Oh. Yeah. I see." Sam didn't see anything, except that the man had a screw loose somewhere.

"Anyway," Glebe said, now in vast good humor, "thank you very much. You've done good work; I can certainly use it. I will take these with me to listen to," he scooped up the compact DAT cassettes. "And I'd like you to carry on taping for a couple more weeks if you would. It's extremely helpful. In the meantime I'll write you a check for your time."

Sam sat up straight with pleasure. "Sure. Thank you."

Glebe fished a couple more blank cassettes out of the soft leather satchel he carried. Sam put them and the recorder into his backpack. "How will you use the sounds?"

"Sometimes they give me ideas. Sometimes I use the tapes themselves in a piece."

"Really?"

Glebe smiled puckishly. "Oh yes. The soundscape becomes quite diverse. Sometimes not at all what a listener might be expecting."

"Wow."

Glebe rose. Sam followed suit. Mr. Carnoostie called, "Don't forget our band practice, Sam."

"I'll try. I have to read this book first." Sam said, forgetting that he was already supposed to have read the book. He was half hoping they'd ask, "What book?" so he could explain his soon-to-be heroism and celebrity, and half hoping they didn't, since he still wasn't sure how Glebe felt about J. Earl.

They didn't ask. Instead, Mr. Carnoostie told the maestro about their new band.

"I once used an ensemble like that in an experimental piece back in the sixties," said Glebe. "In fact, I met one of the musicians again here last fall. During your . . . uh . . . difficulty." He nodded at Sam, who felt himself beginning to blush.

"Carl Gernsbach," supplied Mr. Carnoostie, handily diverting things. "Sure. He's our bassist. The group was called Buzzard Ugly."

"That's it." Glebe's own substantial beak rose and fell. "As I recall, they all wore dresses. I trust you're not going to."

Mr. Carnoostie laughed. Sam didn't. He'd heard enough about dresses today.

"Nah," said Mr. Carnoostie. "We haven't talked about what to wear, but it won't be that. Something lean and mean, right, Sam?"

Sam nodded, trying not to think about either Mr. Carnoostie's substantial middle or the nonexistent physique he stared at in the mirror every morning. He had more time for staring now that he didn't have to share the bathroom with Robin, but no more muscles.

Glebe said, "Is what you call *soul* music popular here?"

"Let's say we're going to broaden some horizons."

Sam slipped away. "Keep on taping," Glebe called after him.

Chapter 26

As usual, he was the first home. He liked being home alone, something that had rarely happened before Robin left. A comforting suppertime smell came from the Crock-Pot as he liberated some cookies from the kitchen. Then he headed to his room to take the first step in becoming a celebrity student for free reading and boyfriend of Delft Hoogstratten.

Flopping on his unmade bed, Sam dug Smitty's battered copy of *Dutch Courage* out of his backpack. The cover showed a German sentry guarding a twilit dock. Three teens, looking much like the Hardy Boys and Nancy Drew, were creeping out from behind some barrels, intent on assaulting him with what was probably a wooden club. It was hard to tell, because someone with a ballpoint pen had transformed it into a male body part, as well as giving everyone mustaches and Martian antennae.

On the back Sam read:

> *"Bless my soul," chuckled stout burgher Van Loon. In the golden lantern glow, he was as round and sturdy as a wooden barrel himself. "If it isn't Hans, and Pieter, and Rulji, too. What brings you out on a night like this?"*
>
> *"Traitors," said Hans fiercely, his eyes glowing like coals. "Where are the guns?"*

A ZESTY, ROLLICKING YARN. AN EPIC ADVENTURE OF DARING AND INTRIGUE! BASED ON A TRUE STORY, HERE IS A GRIPPING TALE FOR READERS YOUNG AND OLD!

Sam sighed. Well, the book looked thin, and the printing was only medium-small. And it was by J. Earl and J. Earl was famous, so it had to be pretty good, *and* it had bits juicy enough to make people mad. He bit into a cookie and started to read.

The story was about three teenagers in German-occupied Holland during the Second World War. The Resistance was relying on smugglers to bring them guns inside barrels of what should have been contraband gin. There was a supposed-to-be-funny old guy and a brutal Nazi colonel who was bald and a smuggler who you knew would be a traitor and a young German soldier a lot like the three Dutch kids and no sex at all. By the time Sam's mom called him down to supper he was beginning a chapter entitled "Guilty Secrets." He went slowly down, feeling the beginning of a new one of his own.

"Well," said Mr. Foster, serving up mashed potatoes as Sam came in, "I see that Finger In the Dike of Decency crowd has got itself back in the paper again, about this book thing." He nodded at the evening's *Eternal* on the kitchen stool. Sam, as usual, had made a point of not reading it. "Seems a couple of trustees are already saying they're in agreement. Now they want the book out of the public library, too."

His parents shook their heads over the trustees. Mrs. Foster summarized their shopping foibles at the Bin. Deep in a Survival Slouch, Sam ate his chicken, then his green beans. Each bite seemed to add to the weight that was already in his stomach.

"The thing of it is," Mr. Foster protested, "these Dike of Decency characters just pull things out of context. We've got one of their handouts in the staffroom, with these one- and two-line quotes. You know: *If God liked Holland, why did he try to drown it?* That kind of thing. *How many Dutchmen can drown in a bottle of gin? Only one; they never share.* It sounds offensive until you see that in the book it's the Nazis that are saying this stuff and you're not supposed to believe them."

"Well, isn't that always the way?" said Mrs. Foster. "See what you want to see, hear what you want to hear."

"Absolutely." Mr. Foster was getting quite worked up. His ponytail was beginning to bob. "And then there's all this nonsense about disrespect to the Dutch Resistance, just because there's a couple of Dutch bad guys as well. No society is homogeneous, for crying out loud. My God, when groups like these FIDOs—"

"FIDODs," Mrs. Foster corrected.

"Whatever. When they get going, alarm bells should go off. That's why it's so important that we get involved. Kids like you especially, Sam, because it's your right to choose to read what they're trying to take away."

"But—" Sam said. He was going to say that he hadn't chosen the book, Mrs. Goldenrod had, but Mr. Foster was on a roll.

"Now, I'm not saying that *Dutch Courage* is a work of art. We're not talking Tolstoy here." Sam caught a look his parents exchanged. "But Sam liked it and he hasn't sunk into moral turpitude or violent anti-Dutch behavior."

"Give him time," said Mrs. Foster. "He's only fourteen."

"Well, these Dike of Decency clowns aren't. Some of them should know better. I mean, B—"

"Enough," Sam's mom cried, raising a hand. "You're not going to be talking to the board; Sam is." She turned to Sam. "Have you decided what *you* want to say?'

"Not exactly." He shoveled in potatoes to avoid saying more. In fact, he'd thought he had decided—until he'd started to read the book. Now things were more complicated.

"Well, it's next Tuesday, don't forget. A little run-through might not be a bad idea." Sam wondered if she was remembering his last appearance before a group of grownups, at town hall. "If you want to talk, we're around."

That, thought Sam, swallowing and adding to the lump in his stomach, was exactly the problem: adults were always around, dragging him into messes like this. "Can I be excused? I have a ton of homework."

He dragged himself back upstairs as if each step was a small Everest. Not even overhearing his mom say "Bert"—Hoogstratten, maybe?—was enough to take his mind off the trouble that lay ahead. In his room, he stalled by quietly picking his guitar. Then he looked up "turpitude." *I wish,* Sam thought. *I haven't even had a date yet.*

Finally he returned to *Dutch Courage,* hoping he'd been wrong the first time. By the time another hour had passed, he knew, with a dreadful sense of finality, that he'd been right. Zesty? Gripping? *Rollicking?* Uh-uh. How could Smitty have enjoyed this? How could Mrs. Goldenrod have assigned it? How could J. Earl have *written* it? With the exception of *A Tale of Two Cities, Dutch Courage* was the worst book Sam had ever tried to read—and next Tuesday he was defending it to the school board.

Chapter 27

Next morning he dragged himself to school in a terrible mood, which did not improve as the day wore on. Darryl got in a couple of unfunny digs about cowgirls. Mrs. Goldenrod asked him if he was prepared for the school board meeting. Then she assigned questions and three more chapters of Dickens. Two periods later, a math test was announced for Monday. Sam's science teacher added a lab report, and pretty soon the homework had piled up like some abominable snowdrift blocking the way to the weekend.

Even worse, rumors of the band and its eccentric membership were the new joke around Hope Springs High. How he could be crazy about a mystery cowgirl *and* in a weirdo gay band was beyond Sam, but it didn't seem to be a stretch for anyone else. At least he hadn't told anyone he'd be talking at the school board. God knew what fun they might have had with that, adding artsy, suck-up browner to the mix.

By lunchtime it was clear that others were feeling the heat too. Amanda said girls were asking her if she was loaning the boys her clothes. Darryl, brandishing a failed math test, noted in a subdued voice that someone had scratched *fag* into the paint on his locker.

"Maybe it's because of your hair," Sam suggested, unable to resist. Darryl had recently attempted to dye his hair a glowing stop-sign red in homage to his current favorite guitarist, Wayne

DeLassie of Atomic Sandpaper. Unfortunately, something had gone wrong and the result was closer to a shocking pink.

"It's not my hair. My hair's red," Darryl insisted, ignoring the evidence. He reached for a cookie that was clearly part of Sam's lunch.

"Hey!" Sam grabbed his wrist.

Some skids pushed by. "No holding hands, girlies."

Sam and Darryl recoiled. Sam looked at the table, then at Darryl, who had shrugged his hoodie up. Darryl looked disconsolately back. They were partners in misery, if not much else anymore.

"Let's get some air," Amanda said. "I've had it in here."

Outside, the usual crowd of skids huddled on the sidewalk across from the school, smoking cigarettes.

"Hey, faggots!" called one. "Where's your dresses?"

"Rock and rollllllll!"

A cold wind pushed them as they stomped across the thin crust of snow on the football field. "Lucky for Delft she's still away," Sam said.

"She's gonna get it when she gets back anyway," Darryl shivered. "In geography today? Like I was joking about how you're in love with Mystery Madison the Country Cutie?"

"Oh, thanks a bunch," Sam sighed.

"Well, I was just joking," Darryl sounded aggrieved. Was he? Sam didn't know. How could Darryl not know he was hurting him, teasing and leaving him out? Darryl went on, "Anyway, these two No Hope girls that were in grade eight with her started saying that that was Delft."

"It was not." Sam and Amanda said at once. They looked at each other.

Darryl didn't notice. "I know. They were just mad at her because they knew I used to like Delft and they're jealous."

Sam stared at Darryl, wondering if he was serious, and, if so, if Darryl was insane. Darryl continued blandly, "Besides, Delft hates country music. And she doesn't look like that, either. Especially in the stacked department."

"That's a piggy thing to say." Amanda looked disgusted.

"Hey, I'm not chasing girls anymore," Darryl proclaimed with more of his usual verve, "so I can say anything I want."

"What are you doing instead?"

"Guitar. I'm going to become a guitar god and then girls will chase me."

"Oh yeah."

Darryl, as usual, was impervious to sarcasm. "Anyway, that's not the point. The point was what they said about me."

"What was that?"

"That they heard we're going to do country in dresses and wigs and they wanted to know my bra size."

"God," said Amanda. "Who cares?"

"I do," exclaimed Darryl. "I don't even have a bra size!"

"Not that, dummy. I mean why don't they give up on the dress thing? All I hear about is Mr. Carnoostie and Sam's dad in dresses and playing in old folks' homes."

"Really?" Sam sighed. "All I hear about is how we all must be gay because Robert and Mr. Gernsbach are."

"That's stupid." Amanda tossed her head. "Neither one of them is gay, and who cares if they were."

"Well," Darryl considered, "maybe not Mr. Gernsbach. He's married, and I've read that, like, some guys just like to—"

"Darryl? Not now, okay?"

Sam could see that Amanda was getting angry, and he wasn't in the mood for one of Darryl's explanations, or even for having to think out his own opinion. As they reached the far side of the field, he stuffed his hands into his jacket pockets and felt the tape recorder.

"I guess we can't quit." Darryl said what they were all thinking.

"We can't quit," Amanda said gloomily. "There's other people counting on us and we're not even really the ones they want to pick on. Besides, we play okay."

"Yeah," Sam agreed reluctantly, "it would be different if we were bad." For a second he wished they were. He pulled out the

tape recorder and turned it on. Clearly and distinctly, he said "Eff."
It seemed to sum things up.

The others looked at him. He held up the recorder. They looked at it.

"Eff," Darryl declared right back.

"Effing something something," Amanda added. The boys were startled. Amanda shrugged sheepishly. They all grinned.

"Something something else!" Darryl crowed.

"Something effing something something something!" from Sam.

"Go something something something!" Amanda again.

"Something!"

"Something!"

"Something even worse!"

They shouted every profanity they could think of into the recorder until Amanda brought them to a halt with a remarkable suggestion involving violence, anatomy, and close relatives. All three of them blushed beyond their wind-reddened cheeks. "Sorry," Amanda said. "I *am* on a hockey team."

"That's okay." Sam switched off the recorder. He felt better as they headed back inside.

The improvement didn't last. Despite it being Friday he felt tired and grumpy and oppressed again by the time he got home. No one had even made Friday night plans. He was hungry and picked on, he had a zit coming up painfully beside his mouth, a pack full of homework, a drum lesson tomorrow that he hadn't practiced for, a deadline to clean up his room, and he was sick of winter already.

And then there was the little matter of *Dutch Courage*, bobbing dangerously on the horizon like a barrel of explosives. What in the world was he going to say that wouldn't make every adult he knew angry with him? Even if he didn't say anything they'd be mad. Faced with this nightmarish tangle of responsibilities, Sam did the only thing that seemed to make any sense: he lay on the den couch and flipped TV channels until he found a sitcom rerun.

The episode was one he'd seen several times before. The predictability was comforting. Why was sitcom life never crappy and complicated? Why did people on sitcoms never have zits? Why did they always have their couch in the middle of the room facing nothing? More to the point, why couldn't his life be like a sitcom?

If it were, the only homework he'd have would maybe be making a tape for O. Sidney Glebe. Or maybe the episode would be about Mr. Gernsbach wearing dresses. And that was all anybody would have to think about as they said funny things on their couch facing nothing. And everything would work out, because nothing really bad ever happened. And if his life were a sitcom he'd already be famous. Although, in sitcom land he technically wouldn't be, because that was supposed to be real life except there wouldn't be a TV show about you, except somehow you'd secretly know that you were famous in kind of a parallel universe sort of way. Or something. Probably. He turned off the TV as the telephone rang.

"Hey, dumb one!" It was Robin. He could hear music in the background, the Dilations, maybe.

"Hi."

"Wow, Mr. Cheerful. Listen, I'm going out to the pub soon, so I wanted to check before I forget: what night is the school board meeting?"

"Tuesday."

"Okay. Tell the parental units I'm coming down for it. I'm going to cover it for my school paper. They love censorship stuff."

"Great. Lucky for them."

"Geez, Sammy, lighten up a little, willya? It's Friday, for God's sake. What's the matter with you?"

A lifetime of experience had taught Sam how risky it could be to confide in your older sister, particularly about things broken, avoided responsibilities, or missing reptiles. Still, these were unusual circumstances, and he had no one else to confide in. Besides, he had the feeling that Robin might understand, about the teasing anyway. She'd spent grade eleven sporting a shaved head on one side, orange spikes on the other, an eyebrow stud, and an assortment of punk regalia. At the time, Sam had sensed this had not always been easy for her, although it had not stopped him from calling her Triceratops Head from time to time. Now he told her a little of what had been going on.

As usual, annoyingly, he had to wait until she stopped laughing. "A dress? *Really?*"

"What I don't get," Sam said, trying to get Robin back on track, "is how all those bozos found out about it. It's not like he wears the stuff in town, or anything." The instant he said it, Sam realized he did know how. He groaned out loud. "Blabbermouth Darryl, it has to be. Who else would be that stupid?"

"Sam, who cares?" Robin said. "The point is, right now, unless you're a puck bunny, it's a dull time of year. There's nothing going on, so they pick on you." Puck bunnies were yet another group at the high school: girls who hung around the arena to be with the hockey players. "But know what? It won't last. It's like you're flavor of the month, except skid attention spans aren't that long. And you're not performing any place, right?"

"Right."

"So in a couple of weeks they'll forget about you. I mean, nobody talks about that stupid crash helmet anymore, right? The one you got stuck in? Or how dumb you looked on TV?"

"NO." He wished Robin would quit bringing those things up.

"See? Now, it would be faster if a puck bunny got pregnant," Robin said. "Hey, see what you can do about it. Anyway, for the school board thing, what were you going to say? Hang on, lemme get my pen. I'll make some notes now."

Sam listened to various rustles and fumblings.

"Okay," Robin said.

"Well, I was going to say I liked it and everything, but that was before."

"Before what?"

Sam hesitated. "Well, before I read the book."

"*Whaaaaat?* You said you'd talk before you read the book? That was pretty stupid. What'd you do that for?"

There was no way Sam was going to admit it was to look good in front of Delft Hoogstratten. He hemmed and hawed about J. Earl and Mrs. Goldenrod and Smitty liking it. "Only now I found out it really sucks but if I say that they'll be mad at me but I can't think of anything good to say about it instead, but I said I'd say something and now they're all saying how great it is that I'm going to, so I have to. Unless"—he had a sudden, hopeful inspiration— "I was sick."

"Yeah, right. Unless it's the plague, it's going to look like you chickened out."

"But they'll be mad at me anyway if I say it's a stupid book."

"Hey," Robin reminded him, "get tough here. You just said you'd talk, you didn't tell them what you'd say. Did you?" For a moment she sounded ominously like their mom.

"No!"

"Then say whatever you want. I mean, this whole thing is about free speech, right? So, you're allowed."

"Yeah, but—"

"And know what?" Robin was warming to her topic. "Nobody's going to care what you say, anyway. It's just like one of my profs was talking about this old chauvinist dude who said that a woman making a speech was like a dog walking on its hind legs: you didn't think about how well they did it, it was cool they did it at all."

"Heyyyy," Sam felt vaguely offended, thought he wasn't sure just how. "I'm not a dog or anything. I'll be sitting down."

Robin sighed on the other end of the line. "Sam, you're a kid. Nobody at the school board pays attention to them, either."

Chapter 28

The phone was long hung up and Sam was still unconvinced by the time his parents got home. His dad mentioned that he'd been talking to Mr. Gernsbach at the school bus pickup: somebody had bashed in their mailbox, which sat on a post at the end of their driveway.

"Why in the world would someone do that?" Mr. Foster wondered. Sam resisted the temptation to say, *Because doughhead Darryl blabbed all over that Mr. Gernsbach is a cross-dresser.* He contented himself with wondering how adults could be so out of it. Then again, his dad wasn't getting teased.

"It's a traditional sport around here," Sam's mom sighed, hanging up her coat. She had a bottle of wine with her. "Not harassing cross-dressers—although that probably would be if there were more of them—bashing mailboxes, I mean. Growing up in the city, you missed out on it." Mrs. Foster had been born and raised in Hope Springs. "You load kids, a case of beer, and a baseball bat into a car or a pickup truck, and you drive up and down the township roads swatting at mailboxes."

"Did you ever do that?" Sam asked.

"No," she said, looking in the kitchen drawer for a corkscrew. "But I know lots who did."

"Anybody I know?"

"Never mind. Most of them have smartened up since. Just remember, Samuel: your generation did not invent stupidity." His mom opened the wine as his dad got out glasses. Sam slunk off to call Steve and Larry and see if they wanted to rent a video.

Saturday morning found him working at the Bulging Bin, washing out plastic buckets that had contained peanut butter and corn syrup. At lunchtime his mom gave him some money and sent him over to Marvin's Family Restaurant. "Get yourself something greasy," she said. "I know you've got homework, and I think Dad is planning Lentils Supreme for dinner."

Outside, Sam looked over at Hoog's Blooms. He'd already checked; Delft wasn't working today. He couldn't accidentally-on-purpose bump into her. He sighed and crossed the deserted entrance to Lint Lane. The classical music had stopped. Looking up, he saw that someone had cut the wires to the speakers. Feeling unable to remain silent himself any longer, he passed Marvin's and continued down the block to the Grandstand. Amanda was there, marking sale price tags for ski jackets.

"Can you get off for lunch?" Sam asked. "I'm going to Marvin's."

"I can't today," Amanda shook her head. "I have to get this done. Anyway, I'm off in another half-hour. Then I'm going to the library."

"Oh. Okay, never mind." He was about to say what was on his mind when Amanda said, "Delft will be glad you kept the secret."

Sam blinked. "You know?"

Amanda shrugged. "Girls talk, boys don't, Sam. Remember?"

Sam remembered. "When did you find out?"

"Back in September when Delft and I got to be friends."

"So like, when I was looking for Madison Dakota and asking questions and everything, you *knew?*"

"Sure. It was funny."

Sam had an instant picture of just how funny it must have been. Clearly this was going to be one of those memories that made him wince, because Amanda said immediately, "But it was kind of sweet, too. It wasn't like you were stomping around drooling or anything. Just all dreamy and trying not to let it show."

Oh great. How reassuring. "But why didn't you guys just tell me?" Amanda crossed off another price with her marker and wrote in a reduced one.

"Well, then I kind of liked you myself—I mean, I still *like* you—but then it was more *like* like, you know? We thought if you liked this girl that didn't even exist, pretty soon you'd get tired of it and smarten up. And anyway, Delft wasn't exactly flattered that you liked this imaginary girl better than her."

Uh-oh. Sam protested, "But, like, as soon as I found out, I started to like—I mean *like* like—Delft. I mean, I like you, too, but, like—" The *likes* in this conversation seemed to be spinning out of control. Sam paused for a breath. "So are you bugged with her now?"

"No. For one thing, it's not like she wants you to like her. And for another," Amanda smiled archly, "I have a mystery admirer."

"Oh yeahh. Do you know who it is?"

The smile again. "I'm working on it."

"Neat," Sam said, feeling as if he was on safer ground again. Not entirely safe; there was something in Amanda's words niggling at him, but safe enough to return to the real purpose of his visit. "Well, I just wanted to tell you that I think I figured out how everybody heard about Mr. Gernsbach."

"Really?" Amanda lowered her marker. For all her practicality, she liked gossip as much as anyone else. Girls talked. "How?"

Sam's face set grimly. "Who knows about Mr. Gernsbach, has a bigger mouth than all the rest of the band put together, and always says stuff without thinking about people's feelings?"

"Darryl did it? Do you know? Did someone tell you?"

"No, but who else could it be?"

"Oh God, that little crud. Boy, if you're right, Sam—"

"Don't say anything to anybody, okay? I just wanted you to know." And Delft, he added silently. Which brought the niggling back, as he turned to go.

"Hey, what do you mean, it's not like Delft wants me to like her? Doesn't she like me?"

"Oh," said Amanda hastily. "Sure she likes you. Why wouldn't she?"

"But does she *like* me?" The *likes* seemed to be starting again.

"What does she say?"

"I don't know. I haven't asked her."

"Maybe you should."

"Yeah, I guess. It's just, you know, difficult. Like you said, guys don't talk."

"I think," Amanda said, a trifle cryptically, "that you should *both* talk."

Chapter 29

Marvin's was warm and bustling. The stools at the counter were full, and the booths were crowded as well. What with the crowd and the unsettled feeling his talk with Amanda had left him with, it took a moment to notice the hand waving from near the back. It was Robert Goodwood, alone. Sam half-heartedly returned the wave and continued to look for a seat. There was nothing. Sam was hungry. He had no choice but to look back at Robert, who gestured him over.

Sam went into Survival Slouch and loped down to the booth, executing a deft slide onto the bench that left him slouching even more. Being seen with probably gay, band nerd, browner, water-walker Robert was not something he felt up to right now.

"Hi," said Robert. He had some sheet music open on the table and a plate of french fries with gravy in front of him. Now he prissily picked up a fry, shook off an excess drop of gravy, and bit it neatly in two. Sam resisted asking him what it sounded like. Despite Robert's apparent fastidiousness, there were a number of sizeable crumbs scattered around the table.

"Hi," Sam replied from somewhere below sea level. He plucked a menu out of the rack and opened it in front of his face before risking a glance around the room. There were a couple of booths full of skids along the opposite wall, but they didn't seem to be paying any attention. Mrs. Marvin came by. Sam ordered a grilled cheese and chocolate milk. Reluctantly putting back the menu, he asked Robert, "Whatcha doing?"

"I'm reading this score for my choir," Robert said. "See who it's by?"

He tilted a sheet toward Sam, who read *O. S. Glebe.* "Hey," Sam said, sitting up a little. Like most people, he had never actually heard anything the nation's most famous composer had composed. "What does it sound like?"

"It's neat. Weird, though. There's no melody, just shifting tones and harmonies."

"Is there a part with fence wire?"

"No, but I read about that. That's in a piece called 'Prairie Prologues,' I think. This is just for voices. We start learning it tomorrow. That's when I'll actually hear it."

"So what did you do, like, play it on the piano or something?"

"No," Robert said matter-of-factly. "I have perfect pitch. I can read the notes and hear them in my head. Or I can hear a note and tell you what it is."

"*Really?* Ho-lee," Sam said, sitting up straighter. "Is that ever cool. *Any* note?"

"Uh-huh." Robert neatly selected his next fry. As he did, something bounced off the saltshaker and landed with a dry *click* on the sheet music. A chunk of toast crumb. Sam stared at it. As he did, a bit of pickle hit his jacket. Startled, he looked around.

"Don't bother," Robert said, brushing off the music. "It's just them. You know who I mean." At the table across the way, the skids were smirking and pretending to mind their own business.

"Geez," Sam said, looking back at Robert. "What'd we do to them?"

"We're breathing, aren't we?"

"Somebody bashed in Mr. Gernsbach's mailbox. I think Darryl blabbed."

"Really? Sometimes," Robert said, chewing, "I hate this place."

A wad of lettuce sailed past. He gathered his music as Mrs. Marvin returned with Sam's order. She looked at the boys, then gave the table a wipe. Sam wanted to explain, but didn't. Adults did not help in these situations. Instead, he listened as Robert talked about music he'd downloaded with the band in mind: Sam Cooke, Ray Charles, Aretha Franklin, Etta James, Wilson Pickett. Sam had heard some of the names, but he didn't know the music. He mentioned his own idea of adding ska music to their repertoire as a few other missiles fell short. Robert nodded enthusiastically as the skids got up to leave. They took the long way out to pass the booth.

"Hey, queer boys!"

"Effin' faggots."

It was too low for anyone but Sam or Robert to hear. Sam scowled and ducked his head. Robert, in his crisp, middle-aged-guy sports shirt, kept his head up, as if they weren't there. Sam sighed as the group jostled its way to the cash up front.

"Imagine what it's going to be like playing anything to them."

"Who cares what they think? We'll be louder."

"Yeah, but—" Sam didn't want to say it, but part of him did care what the skids thought about their music. He wanted everybody to like it. He wanted everybody to like him. He said, "There must be something everyone likes. I don't know, some sound."

Robert shrugged. "Music is what *you* like. If you don't listen, you don't know what you like. *They* don't listen. Too bad for them."

"Yeah, but did you hear those guys? They—"

"I heard them," Robert cut him off. "I listen to everything." He looked at his watch, then tucked the score into the pack on the seat beside him and shrugged on his sensible blue parka. He had a hat and gloves, too.

"You can have the rest of my fries if you want. I have to get going. I'm meeting Amanda at the library to study."

"Really? How come?" Sam asked, meaning why was Robert meeting Amanda. Then again, he thought, lots of gay-type guys hung around with girls. Robert, however, didn't hear the question that way.

"So I can get really good marks," he answered. "So I can get into a really good university, so I can get out of this effing town."

Chapter 30

On Monday, Delft finally returned to school. Sam, still sweating out what he was going to say at the school board, was not in the mood for a heart-to-heart. In any event, Delft was acting distracted herself.

Bad weather forced the cancellation of band practice. Sam was just as glad. In fact, he was hoping the blow would last through Tuesday night as well. Unfortunately, it had pretty much let up by nine o'clock Monday night. J. Earl called to say he'd clear the snow himself; he wanted the exercise. "And don't worry about tomorrow," his voice rasped from the receiver. "I'll carry the ball, you'll be the pretty face. Have you practiced what you're going to say?"

"A little," Sam said.

"Well, as long as you don't kiss the microphone with your forehead again, you'll be fine. It should be a circus. I'll see you there."

The school board offices were in Peterborough, a half-hour from Hope Springs. Sam and his family arrived twenty minutes early and still had trouble finding a place to park. The circus J. Earl had predicted seemed to be in town.

Inside, a crowd milled. TV camera crews were circulating, as well as a small horde of reporters with notebooks and tape recorders. J. Earl, his head shinier than ever under the lights, was holding forth from a spot near the boardroom doors. He was in his customary TV getup of dark slacks and turtleneck, topped with a camel's hair sport coat. He raised an eyebrow in greeting as Sam slouched by in full Survival mode.

TV lights had been set up in the boardroom. There was also a long table, dotted with microphones. Name cards marked the trustees' places. A number of them were already in their seats. Facing the long table was another, smaller table with a single chair and microphone. It had its own special TV light. A few feet behind it sat rows of chairs for spectators, already mostly filled. Sam spotted Mrs. Goldenrod and several other teachers from school. Smitty and Ms. Broom were there too.

The front row was marked with a sign reading SPEAKERS. Several people were already seated there, their backs to Sam.

"That would be you," Mrs. Foster said, nodding.

"Uh-huh." Sam's chin scraped his collar as he nodded. He hadn't worn a collared shirt in some time. He also hadn't felt this nervous in some time: in fact, since the fall fair talent show.

"Are you sure you don't want to talk about what you're going to say?"

"Uh-huh." At the moment, that was about all he *could* say. His laboriously written fifteen-second speech was in his pocket.

J. Earl came bustling up. He waved jauntily to Mrs. Goldenrod, who was waving almost feverishly to him, then turned to Sam. "All set?"

"Uh-huh."

"Good. Now remember: when your turn comes, take your time and talk right into the mike. Come on."

They trooped to the front row and sat down, J. Earl beside a burly man with a jaw-line beard and backswept hair and Sam beside J. Earl. J. Earl turned to the man and Sam, with a start, recognized Mr. Hoogstratten. Sitting on his far side was Delft.

A tide of panic rose. Of course, he realized; the Hoogstrattens were Dutch. They hated the book. Instantly he realized how ridiculous this idea was. The Hoogstrattens, especially Delft, were no dummies.

Except for the silly quotes pulled out to make the book look bad, there was nothing offensive to Dutch people. Was there?

No, they had to be here, like Sam, to support free speech. He looked at J. Earl. The great man was chatting to Hoog Hoogstratten as if they were old buddies. Maybe they were. A dike of relief pushed back the panic tide. Sam flashed a big smile down the row to Delft. She continued staring at the carpet. That was okay, Sam thought, sitting back and feeling a little better. He could understand feeling nervous about speaking.

Beside him J. Earl was burbling, ". . . what you believe in, by golly. But listen, have you done much of this? Then let me give you a little tip: back off from the mike; don't use it at all if you can get away with it. Of course, normally you'd get in close. But this TV stuff makes it a whole other ball game. Their mikes are on a different frequency. Use that one as well and the sound feed for TV will be static—you lose your bigger audience. Plus, the visual is better too. You take a big guy like you hunched over a microphone, it looks uncomfortable, like you need help. You wanta sit back, look confident, talk loud. The picture says here's a guy who's strong, knows his stuff, doesn't need any wussy help. Know what I'm saying?"

Hoog Hoogstratten was nodding, looking both confused and overwhelmed by this celebrity onslaught as the chairman of the school board called the meeting to order. The meeting moved through its opening formalities and regular business before turning to what everyone was waiting for.

"Next," intoned the chairman (who, in fact, was a woman), "the board has before it a request to withdraw from the curriculum the book *Dutch Courage* by J. Earl Goodenough. A number of people wish to speak to this, so we'll accept presentations on the matter now. I'm reminding everyone that they have no longer than ten minutes each." She adjusted her reading glasses and consulted some notes. "We'll begin with the spokesperson for the group that has made this request, the um . . . Finger In the Dike of Decency. Mr. Hoogstratten?"

Hoog Hoogstratten levered himself to his feet. Stunned, Sam turned to Delft. She stared at the carpet. Delft's dad settled himself into the speaker's chair. He spread papers on the table in front of him. The TV lights came on. Life had never seemed as unfair as it did at this moment, not even the Christmas Robin had gotten a green bicycle with handlebar streamers and he hadn't gotten a Hug Me Herman because Santa didn't make enough. Nothing compared with the disaster that was about to overtake him. After Delft and her dad finished complaining about *Dutch Courage*, Sam's speech was going to leave him about as popular with them as plastic flowers. How did he ever get into this?

Mr. Hoogstratten put on his half-glasses and squinted into the glare. Then, hands planted on the table, he leaned toward the mike and cleared his throat. The resultant electronic rumble sounded like a motorcycle gang revving up in Lint Lane.

"Back off," hissed J. Earl. "I told you."

The Hoogster twitched, turned his head slightly, and nodded. He was pink from his beard to the roots of his DA hairdo. The lights were already warming up the room.

"Mr., ah, Mrs. Chairman . . . person," he bellowed, well away from the mike, "and members of the board. The Finger In the Dike of Decency. Believes there. Is nothing. More precious. Than the hearts. And minds. Of our young people." His head bobbed up and down as he tried to read and look at the board members at the same time. He reminded Sam of an enormous version of the plastic dogs you sometimes saw bouncing their heads in the rear windows of cars, the ones whose eyes blinked as turn signals. His straining voice, on the other hand, had the volume and charm of a rusty chainsaw.

"They are impressionable. And there cannot be any room. In what they read. For. Ethnic. Slurs. Or deliberate lies. About any of the peoples. That help make this—"

"Mr. Hoogstratten?" It was the chairman. "Sorry to interrupt. It might be easier for you to speak into the microphone."

"Huh? But—" The Hoogster's head bobbed and again he almost turned to J. Earl, who hissed, "Halfway, halfway," then leaned over to Sam and whispered, "Bingo. This guy is toast. Lesson in celebrity, Foster: someone you've seen on TV fusses over you, you want to believe it, especially if you thought you wouldn't like them. Now he's totally confused."

Sure enough, Hoog Hoogstratten bent stiffly forward, about halfway to the microphone. The new posture kept him from yelling loud enough, but he wasn't close enough to the microphone for it to help.

"Sorry, Mr. Hoogstratten, could you speak up a bit?"

"Pardon?"

"Speak up, please."

Frustrated, Delft's dad leaned in close. "IS THIS BETTER?" People winced and covered their ears as feedback squealed through the room. The Hoogster lurched back. Sam couldn't see much of his face, but what he did see was red now and beading with sweat. Clearly Hoog Hoogstratten didn't enjoy public speaking any more than Sam did. Sam felt a small pang of kindred pain. He squirmed in his chair and looked at the carpet. It was embarrassing watching an adult be embarrassing. He didn't dare look at Delft. Sam knew from personal experience the tribulation of having a dad who behaved like a total doofus in public. And now, he was part of the team that was making Delft's dad look like one too.

He snuck a glance at J. Earl. The great man was sitting composedly, listening as if Mr. Hoogstratten were flawlessly delivering an interesting speech on shade gardening. *Oh yeah,* Sam thought angrily. The Hoogster was toast all right—and so was Sam Foster.

Mr. Hoogstratten stumbled on, talking about the contributions the Dutch had made to Canada and their sacrifices during the war, and reading out some of the offending passages. By the time he got to the end, he was doing somewhat better, but by then, Sam sensed, it was too late; the room was restless. Not even applause from FIDOD supporters could disguise it.

"Mr. Hoogstratten, have you read the whole book?" asked a board member.

"No, and I'm not going to, either. What I read was bad enough."

This statement earned him another round of applause. The chairman called for order, thanked Delft's dad, and called on J. Earl Goodenough. The two men passed on their way to and from the speaker's chair. J. Earl said, "Tough luck. It's tricky, isn't it?" Mr. Hoogstratten started to nod, then started to glare, then looked just plain confused and unhappy. Sam, still embarrassed for him, looked away as he sat down.

J. Earl plopped himself briskly down in front of the microphone and pulled it close. With the lights reflecting off his head, he intoned, "Madame chair." It sounded like the voice of God coming through the speakers. "I'll be brief. Thy two breasts are like two young roes that are twins, which feed among the lilies."

Somebody gasped. The chairman—woman—sat upright. J. Earl, the old smoothie, shot an admonishing finger in the air and balanced the silence in the room on its tip.

"Poetry buffs and churchgoers," he went on in his more familiar growl, "will recognize the Bible: Song of Solomon, chapter four, verse five. Having quoted the Bible, for a reason, I've got three other words to say: freedom, responsibility, and context.

"If words from the Bible shock you, maybe it's because you're hearing them on their own, out of context, in the wrong place and time. If someone pulls out words I wrote as speech for a Nazi character and reads 'em off as if I spouted them on the street corner, they're pulling the same trick. And since I lied about my age to join the navy and fight the buggers, that tees me off.

"Part of that fight was to have the freedom to read whatever we want. Every freedom comes with a responsibility. Here it's the responsibility to think about what you're reading. I'm not supposed to do it for you, dammit. Writers are a tricky bunch; they're fond of irony. That's a fourth word. I'll leave it for some people here to look up, but here's a hint: if a bigoted idiot has a speech in a book, maybe the truth is the opposite of what he's saying. Hell, there's people won't believe anything *I* say, so why believe one of my characters?

"Now, the last time I checked, we were supposed to be teaching kids *how* to think, not *what* to think. If you think the kids in this room tonight can't think for themselves, *you've* got another think coming. Thank you."

With that, the great man rose and stalked back to his seat. Perhaps inflated by indignation, real or feigned, he looked somehow a foot taller than he actually was. Mrs. Goldenrod was on her feet instantly, leading the applause. There was less than there had been for Mr. Hoogstratten—FIDOD clearly had more supporters in the room—but it was far more enthusiastic.

"See how I set you up there?" J. Earl whispered, settling back in his chair. "Now you'll look like a freethinking genius. Just remember to do what I told you."

Sam nodded tightly as Delft was called on to speak. He did not feel like a freethinking genius. He felt like a trapped kid and he was angry about it.

"If you had that stuff to say, what'd you have to make him"— he nodded at Delft's dad—"look dumb for?"

J. Earl turned and raised a merry eyebrow. "We're playing hardball here, Foster. The barbarians are at the gates. You're not going soft on me now, are you?"

"No."

Delft sat in front of the microphone. Perhaps being more used to microphones, she didn't look as uncomfortable as her father had. On the other hand, she didn't look happy, either.

"Who the hell is this?" whispered J. Earl. Clearly he was feeling feisty after his performance.

"My girlfriend." This was not true, of course, but Sam, in the midst of his anger, was beginning to feel a kind of damn-the-torpedoes determination that could make anything happen.

"Lucky dog. So, she's on our side."

"The guy you tricked," Sam hissed back fiercely, "is her dad."

"Ah," said J. Earl, "another airhead. Sorry."

Sam flicked a glare at J. Earl, then turned to watch Delft, who, in a flat, small voice far from her singer's tones, read out: "I started to read this book and didn't want to finish it because it was offensive to my Dutch heritage. I was insulted. My grandpa fought against the Germans and made many sacrifices. He says he didn't know any traitors like the ones in the book, so I think the book must be wrong, because he was there. Also, it is not right that Dutch people are cowards and drink too much gin. Not even the part about growing tulips was right. I know, because we have a flower business.

"I think that instead of this we should read books that make us feel good about ourselves and teach us things. Thank you."

Down she sat, to more plaudits from the Dike of Decency. The board listened to several more complaints about *Dutch Courage,* as well as defenses from a librarian and a retired radio announcer. None of them, it turned out, had read the whole thing. Sam began to wonder darkly if anyone but he, J. Earl, and Smitty ever had. Then it was his turn.

He could feel the pressure of eyes on him as soon as he stood up. It didn't matter. Still filled with his newfound determination, he folded himself down in front of the microphone and brushed the hair back from his eyes. In this chair the lights were even brighter, and it was quite hot. He pulled his speech from his pocket, but didn't unfold it.

Before him, several board members were jotting notes. Several others leaned back, chins on chests, gazing at him with rapidly glazing eyes, and the remainder sat in the overly expectant attitudes grownups adopted for children who announced they knew a joke. Sam was reminded of his talk with Robin. Right now she was somewhere behind him. As he leaned in to the microphone he wondered if she was taking notes. Well, she'd better be, because *he* didn't have whatever was coming next written down. He was also reminded of Robert, for some reason; maybe because he was about to win an unpopularity contest.

He opened his mouth, then stopped.

"Go ahead, Mr. Foster," the chairman encouraged.

"I was just waiting for them to stop writing," Sam said, "so they could listen to me, too."

The words rang out over the sound system in a voice that was not his own. He paused, astonished at his own rudeness. Two of the trustees hastily put down their pens. One wrote on for a moment.

"I'm sure Mr. Simmons can hear you as well," said the chairman, "and we don't want to waste your time."

"I'm not talking about hearing," Sam said. "I'm talking about listening. And that's okay, I won't take long." *Where was this coming from,* part of his brain wondered. Another part said, *Alllll riggght.* A third said, *You're dead.*

The trustee put down his pen. He crossed his arms and looked at Sam. He smiled slightly, but his eyes were saying, *Okay, smart boy.*

"Gee, thanks," Sam said. If he was already dead, what did it matter? "See, my sister, who's pretty smart, said it wouldn't matter what kids said here, because it would be like talking dogs or something, just weird that they do it at all." He heard a ripple of confused laughter. He knew he'd gotten the quote wrong. It only made him push on more fiercely.

"But everybody wants me to say something, so I don't know, maybe she's wrong. I do know I read the whole book, so I found out something nobody else did: it was really bad. It was so bad it almost made *Tale of Two Cities* look good, except it was shorter. You could guess everything, and the kids weren't like real kids. They didn't talk right or anything. And when we write, our teacher says we're not supposed to use clichés like 'suddenly' and 'muscles like iron' because it's sloppy writing? Well, it's *full* of that sloppy writing. It was also totally boring and I'd never, like, *choose* to read it."

There, that was one thing off his chest. Sam paused for a breath and a trustee opened her mouth to speak. Sam shot up a finger the way J. Earl had. It worked. *Oh wow,* part of his brain said into the silence.

"But. You can't just, like, ban it because it su—because it's bad. I mean, I even know a guy who liked it. *And* it isn't mean to Dutch people. If you read the *whole thing,* they're the heroes in the end, except for the one traitor guy, and there have to be bad Dutch people too. I mean, there just do. Sorry.

"So, since I got asked to talk, I think it should be that anybody who wants to can read it, but don't make us study it because it's not worth it."

There was a pause, or maybe it was a stunned silence. A trustee asked, "What do you think would be good enough?"

"Um . . ." Sam hated questions like this. It was the same as being asked your favorite bands; you always went blank and thought of everyone you wanted to mention later. He grasped at the only name that popped up from a recent conversation. *"War and Peace?"*

"I see." The trustee made a note. "Is that what you like to read?"

"Well," Sam said, "mostly I like *Mad* magazine. And the cartoons in the *New Yorker.*"

There were no further questions. Having managed to say things that would offend the school board, the Hoogstrattens, Mrs. Goldenrod, Smitty, and J. Earl, and embarrass Robin and his parents, all on TV, Sam returned to his chair.

Chapter 31

His damn-the-torpedoes attitude evaporated the second his bottom reconnected with his chair. What had he done? It felt as if an imposter had taken his place up there. Sam stared at the flag, so he wouldn't have to see anybody glaring at him.

The chairperson declared the board would go in camera for private discussion. Spectators would have to leave the room. A buzz of conversation rose. Sam leapt to his feet for a quick exit. Unfortunately, the retired radio announcer was blocking his path. Before he could dodge through the chairs, he felt a dig in the ribs, and the oddness began.

"Bang on, Foster," J. Earl's voice chuckled below his ear. "You've been going to school on me. I've gotta hand it to you: saying you hated it was a damn good touch. I almost believed it myself. Made it sound as if you weren't some butt-kissing sycophant. I told you I'd make you look like a freethinking genius."

"What?" Sam turned.

"You were on thin ice with *suddenly*, though. I never use the word."

Before Sam could respond, J. Earl had wheeled to talk to a reporter.

Not knowing what to make of this, Sam pushed his way through to his parents. "I want to go now."

"Sounds good to me," said his mom, picking up her jacket and Sam's.

"Right on," Mr. Foster rose. They were both looking at him a little oddly, but then why wouldn't they?

"I'll be at the door." Sam grabbed his jacket and hurried ahead.

His parents and Robin stepped out into the cold a few minutes later. They walked to the car in silence. Finally, his mom said, "Well, dear, good for you. You certainly spoke your mind."

"Hey, they were being rude to Sam, too," Robin put in.

"That's true," admitted Mrs. Foster. "Good point. It just didn't sound like Sam, somehow." She turned in the front seat. "Did you plan to say all that?"

"Um, not exactly that way."

"Well, I thought it was a really gutsy performance," said his dad, the drama teacher. "Standing up for a book you didn't like—God, that's tough. But why didn't you tell us you didn't like it? We only encouraged you because we thought it was a book you cared about."

"Aw, well, you know, I thought everybody else liked it." He prayed Robin didn't leap in with a "He didn't know because he hadn't read it!" It would be just like her.

Robin looked out the window.

"Oh geez, Sam. Really?" their dad said. "Gosh, I'm sorry. I didn't say anything because I thought *you* liked it. *Dutch Courage* is one of those clunkers that they shoved into the curriculum back when there wasn't much else Canadian to read. It's a definite turkey. Just between us, I think the only reason Elvira Goldenrod keeps teaching it is that she's got a bit of a thing for J. Earl Goodenough."

"Huh?" Sam's mouth was open.

"Unrequited, of course. But there hasn't been a Mr. Goldenrod around since—"

"Nineteen-seventy," supplied Mrs. Foster, keeper of Hope Springs' lore. "They were both hippies. Word was they split after a three-day acid trip."

Sam spent the remainder of the drive trying to envision Mrs. Goldenrod as a flower child. It was a tough stretch. To complete his befuddlement, Robin draped an arm over his shoulders as they trooped into the house. "Sammy," she whispered gleefully, "you were effin' great."

The school board meeting made the late local news on two TV channels. Mostly the footage was of J. Earl, but there was a bit of Sam, too. He was shocked by how thin he looked. One report showed him saying the book shouldn't be offensive to the Dutch, the other ran a snippet of him saying it stunk.

"Well," his dad laughed, "now the world knows where *you* stand."

"Gotta like that quote selection," Robin deadpanned. "Remind you of anyone?"

The announcer closed the item by saying, "And this just in: the school board has apparently voted not to ban the book."

"Yippee," Mr. Foster yawned, flicking off the set. "Score one for free speech."

The next day was no less disconcerting. Fortunately, none of Sam's friends were TV news watchers, but there were the small matters of Delft and Mrs. Goldenrod to contend with. How would he ever pass English if Mrs. Goldenrod had it in for him? What if Delft quit the band and never spoke to him again, just when Amanda had suggested they talk? He slouched to school with the traitorous Darryl, who he supposed he should avoid for his betrayal of Mr. Gernsbach. Right now, it was too much to contemplate. Darryl's droning about a new picking technique his guitar teacher was showing him allowed Sam to skirt his worries, like a postman easing past a snoozing pit bull. As they reached the school, though, Sam saw the *Hoog's Blooms* van pulling out of the parking lot, and the dog awoke.

"What would we do if Delft quit?" Sam interrupted.

"I dunno." Darryl shrugged. "Put Robert in a dress, I guess. Why would she quit?"

"I think she's mad at me for something I said."

"What?"

"Never mind."

Mrs. Goldenrod looked about as far from hippiedom as it would be possible to get when Sam went into class. He'd purposely waited until one second before the bell rang to slip into the room, although this had made it trickier to also avoid Delft, who had clearly been stalling also. In her typically starchy way, Mrs. Goldenrod announced that the ban on *Dutch Courage* had been lifted, but that it was too late; they would continue to study *A Tale of Two Cities*. Everyone groaned, but then they would have groaned if she'd said they were going back to *Dutch Courage,* too. It wasn't until everyone was leaving, with homework, that she beckoned Sam to her desk.

"You made an interesting presentation last night, Sam."

"Um, thanks." *Interesting* was the key word here. It was the kind of polite starter teachers liked to use before ripping you to shreds.

"And I had a talk with Earl Goodenough last night, too. I think the problem is that you're too young for the book, really. Maybe I should save it for grade twelve. The clichés are part of an elegiac quality that adds poignancy to what really is a passionate lyricism that—well, anyway, I asked you to speak your mind and you did, very forcefully. So, to say thanks, these are for you." Reaching down, she produced a stack of worn paperback books and handed them to Sam. He looked: *Inside Mad, The Brothers Mad, Mad Strikes Back, Son of Mad.*

"Oh, wow."

"Vintage Mad, the best they ever did. I bought them back in the early sixties, when I was your age, about the time I first read *Dutch Courage*—and that other one there."

Sam riffled past the *Mad*s to the much thicker book beneath. *War and Peace.* Leo Tolstoy. He gulped, mentally. Mrs. Goldenrod said, "I always remember Prince Andrey lying on the field at Austerlitz, watching the clouds roll by. I used to go out and do that. Despite your suggestion, I doubt we'll be reading it in school."

"Thanks, Mrs. Goldenrod, but I can't take all your books." Especially big thick ones with tiny printing.

"Sam, stories are like music. They're for sharing, not owning. I've read them a million times. Enjoy. Now get going or you'll be late."

He stumbled off, more mixed up than ever.

Chapter 32

Delft avoided him all day. This left Sam with a knot in his stomach only slightly smaller than the one he got when he thought about talking to her. He tried to undo both by concentrating on what to do about Darryl.

Any guy that went around sticking helmets on people's heads, leaving them out of invitations, trying to grab girls when the lights went out, and ratting out cross-dressers in his own band had to be dealt with. Darryl was a pain. And a bore, always blabbing on as if he knew everything in the world and then laughing about how he was practically flunking out. God! What was wrong with the guy, Sam wondered, as he doodled his way furiously through geography. What had happened to the Darryl he used to know, back in grades four and five and six? The guy who always used to phone him to do stuff? Who always shared gum and candy? Why couldn't Darryl be more like his brother? Man, if Darryl had half Ryan's talent, or even just tried as hard, ADHD could have been great. Well, Sam thought, the free ride was over. Tonight, at the makeup practice, he was going to say a few things. If they needed to get a new guitarist afterward, well, there were lots around.

Sam stared at the headrest of the seat in front of him, about where his dad's ponytail would be, all the way to Gernsbach's. Darryl's offer of gum was virtuously refused. Mr. Carnoostie's headlights picked out the battered mailbox as they turned in the drive.

Mr. Gernsbach, in gray warm-up pants and his Grateful Dead sweatshirt, was already in the rehearsal shed. His parrot was perched on his amplifier, a new touch; the golden retriever lay nearby. As the door opened, the dog raised its head.

"Walkies, Whiskey?" croaked the bird. "Walkies, walkies?"

The dog scrambled up eagerly.

"No walkies, no walkies," cackled the bird. The dog drooped again.

Sam was perched nervously behind his drum kit by the time Delft arrived with Amanda and Robert. She avoided his eye as they took their coats off. Okay, Sam thought, at least she was here. Maybe she'd think better of him after he bravely unmasked Darryl. Before he could think anymore, Mr. Gernsbach asked for everyone's attention. First he introduced the parrot as Otis. Then: "I guess you saw the mailbox. I don't know if you saw the spray paint on the road. And I've heard the kids on my school bus, too. This kinda thing pops up for me every few years, someone starts a rumor, you know."

Yeah, thought Sam, don't we all wonder who? He glared at Darryl. The effect was somewhat spoiled by Darryl not noticing. He looked to Amanda for support. She gave him a hard look back. What was that about? Mr. Gernsbach went on, "Anyway, I just wanta say that I can handle it, but if it's bothering you guys, it's cool if you want me to bow out. I don't want anybody else having a hassle."

Before Sam could even open his mouth, Robert said, "No way. Nobody's pushing us around."

"Right," said Amanda. A general rumble of agreement followed.

"I just wish we knew what idiot started it, Carl," someone said.

This was it: D-Day for Darryl. Sam stood up. "I—"

Mr. Gernsbach raised his hand. "Listen, there's lotsa people know. I don't keep it the world's biggest secret. Somebody says something at a coffee shop, on the bus, you know. The kids get started. Anyway, it's done. C'mon, let's play." He flipped the power switch on his bass amp. Sam turned on his drum stool and saw Delft staring at him, white-faced.

They worked over two or three tunes for the better part of an hour before calling a break. Mr. Gernsbach took the pets back in the house. Delft slipped outside. Robert and Amanda were huddled at the keyboard with Mr. Carnoostie. Darryl was fiddling with his amp. Darryl or Delft, which would it be? Sam headed outside.

The night was windless and clear. This far from town you could see the stars with startling clarity. Delft was looking up at them, hugging herself against the cold. Sam's sneaker crackled through the ice crust on a puddle. She turned.

"Oh Sam, thank goodness. Should we tell him about us?"

"Who? What about us?" What flitted nonsensically through his brain was, "That we're going out?"

"Mr. Gernsbach. That it was *us*. Don't you remember?"

"What?"

"That day when we went around taping. Remember? We went to Marvin's for hot chocolate and we were joking about Mr. Gernsbach. You know? The balloons? *Pop?* And the skids came in and they *heard*. It's all our fault."

Sam had a brief, terrible, elevator-stomach sensation as the scene came back to him. As they'd left, some goof had tried to startle them.

"Should we tell him?" Delft said again.

"No!" Sam blurted. He was trembling. He felt as if he was backing away from something, the edge of a cliff, perhaps, just revealed in a flash of lightning. "No. Like Mr. Gernsbach said, it doesn't matter. It would have come up somehow or other anyway."

"But Amanda said you thought it was Darryl."

"I know. I was wrong. I'll, like, tell everyone."

"I already told Amanda. She told Robert."

"Oh, God. Did anybody tell Darryl?"

"What you thought? No. Amanda was going to rip his head off until I told her and she told Robert. So now she just thinks you're stupid."

"Oh." This did not make him feel as much better as he had hoped. He asked what he had to ask. "Do *you* think we should tell Mr. Gernsbach?"

"Uh-huh."

"I guess you're right. It was just that I've already gotten in enough trouble by talking."

"Well, me too."

"How do you mean?"

"How do *you* mean?" asked Delft.

"You know, last night. Now you're mad at me and your dad is mad at me and—"

"I'm not mad at you," said Delft. "I thought you'd be mad at me for saying that stuff."

"I'm not mad at you."

"Oh, thank God. I was so scared about what you'd say that I kept avoiding you."

"Ohhhh, I thought—"

"No, listen," Delft interrupted. "I didn't want to. I felt so stupid, but Daddy made me. I mean, I didn't even read the book."

Anxiety was sliding from Sam like snow off a roof. "Really?" he said expansively, "Well, I almost di—" He stopped, deciding to quit while he was ahead. Delft, anxious to confess all, was already plowing on.

"I mean, if old Mrs. Doberman hadn't told Daddy about it in the first place, he never would have known. I don't know how she found out."

"Because we were all talking about it," said Sam, remembering kissing day at the theater, "back when we were decorating that Christmas tree."

"Oh, God," Delft groaned. "So that's our fault too."

"No, it isn't. It's Mrs. Doberman's. Anyway, I'm sorry if your dad is mad now."

"No, no," Delft said. "He isn't mad either. He thinks you're on his side because you said you didn't think it should be taught in school. He thought you were great."

Sam paused to absorb this further reversal. By now, he was becoming philosophical about the various things people seemed to believe he had said. J. Earl thought he'd faked his distaste. Robin and his parents wondered if he'd planned to be rude. The TV news made him sound alternately like a lover or a hater of the book. Mrs. Goldenrod believed he wanted to read Tolstoy, and Mr. Hoogstratten, that he wanted *Dutch Courage* banned. Had they only heard what they wanted? Wasn't anybody *listening?* On the other hand, just what the heck had he said?

It was too cold to ponder the questions. And right now, who cared anyway? He hadn't blabbed too much about Darryl. He could apologize to Mr. Gernsbach. Somehow he had emerged from the book hassles better off than ever. Inside, he could hear piano chords and Robert la-la-ing a melody. Delft was still in the band, and she was looking at him with a friendly light in her eye, an admiring light, a—gulp—*romantic* light.

Sam realized they were kind of sort of leaning toward each other, their foreheads in danger of clonking. *What the hey,* thought Sam, closing his eyes. He was prepared to live dangerously. He could feel the warmth of Delft's toothpastey breath as he tried a tentative pucker, leaned farther—and was jolted back by a horrendous squawk. It had come from inside. Delft ran to the door, Sam following.

Robert stood at a microphone looking alternately pleased and alarmed. Everyone else was looking at him. Sam plucked at Darryl's sleeve. "What happened?"

"Ho-lee," Darryl said in awed tones, never taking his eyes off Robert. "I think his voice has broken."

Chapter 33

January cold inched into February cold. Robin came home for her university reading week. Sam didn't notice her doing any reading, unless she did it in the bathroom, which she instantly hogged again, but she did show him a picture. Reprinted from an old newspaper, it showed a grinning bulldog of a man in a boxy double-breasted suit and a garish tie, with a Santa hat perched on the back of his crew-cut head. He was posed with two boys in knickers and kneesocks, looking self-conscious beneath their plastered-down hair, their dress-up collars and ties askew. Each was holding what appeared to be a small, gift-wrapped Christmas present. *F. Xavier Muldoon,* read the cutline beneath the picture, *with youngsters at his Christmas party at the Knights of Columbus hall, Saturday last.*

"It's Xavier the Savior," said Robin. "The hockey guy J. Earl was talking about. I'm doing my sports profile on him. He grew up in this neighborhood called Cabbagetown, which was pretty tough, and every year he'd go back there and have a Christmas party with presents for all the kids. This picture is from 1937. Notice anything about the kids?"

"Not really." Sam put down his guitar and squinted at the grainy reproduction. If you got past the old-fashioned clothes and hair, they were pretty average, maybe nine or ten years old, both kind of skinny. The shorter one had a cocky tilt to his head. The way he bit back on his grin made him look as if he were savoring some private joke. The other boy smiled artlessly beneath a long nose.

"Too bad," said Robin. "Because there's two kids quoted in the article that went with the picture. Their names are Sidney Glebe and Earl Goodenough."

"Whaat? Really?" Sam stared again at the photo. The tilt and grin refocused themselves into faint tracings of J. Earl on TV. The other boy's long nose suddenly had beak potential. "Oh, yeahhh. Look at that."

"Uh-huh. I've been trying to reach them for quotes."

"Well, I know J. Earl has gone back to Mexico," Sam said. The great man had departed immediately after setting up a spring lecture tour on censorship. "Maybe O. Sidney Glebe went there too."

"I heard they can't stand each other," Robin said.

Sam nodded, belatedly remembering something he'd been supposed to ask J. Earl. "Did the article say anything about a black spot?"

"Huh?"

"The black spot," said Mr. Foster, cruising through the family room with a basketful of laundry, "was what the pirates in *Treasure Island* would slip you if you were sentenced to die." He passed through the doorway, his unpiratical ponytail following.

"Thanks, Dad," they both called, and shook their heads. Parents.

Robin returned to university and Sam to the daily grind of homework, practice, chores, and video gaming. The band continued to chug along as the snow began to melt, more or less forgotten around town by now. Robin had been right. The spotlight had faded when a puck bunny had indeed become pregnant—no thanks to Sam. He and Delft had apologized to Mr. Gernsbach, privately, and tried to help him repair his mailbox. Mr. Gernsbach had generously accepted both the apology and the attempted help, which had probably stretched out the job. Then he'd given them a lift back into town, to the post office, where Delft had another airmail letter to send off to a friend in Holland.

"Like a pen pal?" Sam had asked.

"Sort of," she'd replied.

Musically, things were going pretty well. The band had nine songs. Sam's drum teacher said all the playing had vastly improved his skills. Robert's voice was creeping back under control, although it still did refreshingly odd things from time to time. It sounded as if he was eventually going to be able to replace Mr. Foster on some vocals. Also improved, though Sam didn't like to admit it, was Darryl's guitar playing. One night, both Mr. Gernsbach and Sam's dad had complimented it.

This helped the band, but it secretly annoyed Sam. Learning that Darryl had not been guilty of ratting out Mr. Gernsbach and that he himself was to blame had not made Darryl more likeable. In some obscure way it all still seemed to Sam to be Darryl's fault, even though the guy was, in fact, not being as much of a pain. Gum was being shared. Even better, Darryl, for once true to his word, had gotten a musical side project going, a goth metal band with Larry and two others from his gym class. While this meant listening to a lot of talk about studded dog collars and fog machines, it was better than teasing about Madison Dakota. Best of all, they practiced Saturday nights, which meant that one night per weekend Darryl wasn't everyone's social gatekeeper.

Really, the only thing that hadn't improved was Sam's romance with Delft—if you could call hanging out with her and all their friends, three sisterly hugs, and once sharing a ride to band practice a romance. Except for a few lunches at Marvin's on days when they were both working, there never seemed much opportunity to be alone with her. Twice he'd invited her to movies before the whole group made plans, but both times she'd been busy. Each time he'd been surprised to find himself more relieved than disappointed.

As spring became a reality the skids came drifting back to Lint Lane, waging a guerilla war against classical music by recutting the speaker wires each time they were repaired. Mrs. Foster disgustedly reported that the Downtown Business Association was now talking about a video surveillance camera.

Robin returned for the summer in early May. She had received an A for her profile of F. Xavier Muldoon. She had also made two copies. One was for J. Earl, who was off on his lecture tour. The other Sam gave to O. Sidney Glebe when he finally turned in his tape recorder and cassettes. Mr. Carnoostie was already busy helping to organize some local musicians for Glebe, who wanted to begin rehearsals on parts of the *Hope Springs Suite.* Mrs. Doberman had announced to the paper that its premiere would be on Canada Day, July 1st.

All of which inevitably led to Smitty, because the Yeswecan service club always organized Hope Springs's Canada Day festivities, including the fireworks and the demolition derby. As he dropped Sam off at the Goodenoughs' for a spring yard cleanup, Smitty asked the fateful question.

"Are you guys still playing in that band?"

"Uh-huh," Sam said, a little surprised that Smitty even remembered. The band was still rehearsing, but they hadn't come close to playing anywhere but in Mr. Gernsbach's shed.

"Good," Smitty said. "So listen, I've got to get some bands to play in the park Canada Day afternoon. Do you guys want to be one of them?"

Sam froze. Misunderstanding his hesitation, Smitty said, "We'll pay and everything. I know there's a lot of you, but don't worry."

It wasn't that. All his January fears had come swirling back, not to mention the others he'd had all the way back at the talent show. What if they got booed offstage by skids looking for Mr. Gernsbach in a dress? What if Mr. Gernsbach *wore* a dress—particularly the floral print? What if Sam missed his fills on "Midnight Hour" or if Robert's voice cracked or Darryl did those stupid windmill strums or Mr. Foster wore a tuxedo?

On the other hand, what if they were great? They'd done all that practicing. What if everybody loved them, if they blew the skids right out of the park? They'd be stars. And in the excitement of the moment, as they basked in an ovation, maybe Delft would turn to him and—Sam looked at Smitty, who was once again wearing his BALD ON TOP cap. "I'll ask," he said. "We've got a practice tonight."

"Okay, just let me know soon. I wanta get this done, 'cause this Canada Day thing is turning into a nightmare. I've gotta talk to this Glebe guy about what he needs for his show, and Mrs. Doberman says the fireworks have to begin exactly as he finishes *and* she wants the demo derby canceled, so the noise doesn't interfere with this Glebe guy's music."

"Whaaaat?" Sam was shocked. Canceling the demolition derby was like, well, canceling the Stanley Cup playoffs. In fact, these days, they both seemed to finish at about the same time. "You can't cancel the derby. It's like the most popular thing in town."

"You can if you're paying for the fireworks."

"Huh?"

"Mrs. Doberman is paying for the fireworks. You have to have those on Canada Day, too."

"So don't let her pay."

"We have to, Sam. You know what fireworks cost? They're expensive. Our show runs about ten thousand dollars. Usually the Yeswes can raise that and more, but it's been a bad winter for bingos. We just don't have the money. So Mrs. Doberman's offered to pay, but only if we do things her way. And that means dumping the derby."

"Wow," said Sam. "People aren't going to be happy when they find out."

Smitty smiled glumly. "Tell me about it," he said.

Chapter 34

Sam announced Smitty's offer at rehearsal that evening. By now they were practicing with the shed doors open to the mild evenings. The cheer that went up was loud enough to bring Mrs. Gernsbach out to see what was going on.

When the hubbub died down, Mr. Carnoostie reminded everyone that something remained to be done before they could perform. "We haven't got a name yet. What are we going to call ourselves?"

Discussion followed, featuring vastly different ideas: The Empty Calories, Ace High and the Blackjacks, Born Yesterday, The Tightly Wound Springs, The Mojos, Angry Lips, Late For Dinner, Six String Razors From Hell. One by one they were rejected.

"Look at it this way," Mr. Foster suggested. "The kind of music we play isn't exactly Canadian, but we are, and we've tried to give it our own twist, right? So the name should imply that somehow, and it should say *power* too. You know, 'we'll blow your socks off' kind of thing. *And* maybe be a little bit retro."

"The Canadian Tires."

"The Doughnuts."

"The Timbits."

"Walkies, Whiskey, walkies?" This was not a suggestion; it was Otis the parrot interrupting. The dog scrambled up. Mr. Gernsbach hushed Otis and perched it on his shoulder. Its plumage was nicely set off by his simple black shift.

"Group of Seven," Mr. Foster got them back on track.

"There's nine of us."

"Oh yeah."

"The Curling Stones."

"They're rocks."

"Okay: Cold Rocks."

"The Maples."

"Maple Leafs."

"Maple Rockers."

"It's not rock, though."

"Yeah, but—"

"Maple Nitro," said Sam. The phrase had bubbled up unexpectedly from somewhere. There was a pause.

"Hey."

Heads nodded. "Not bad."

"Nitro instead of syrup," said Mr. Foster slowly. "I like it. All in favor?"

Everyone was, except Darryl, who still leaned toward Six String Razors From Hell.

"Call your other band that," suggested Amanda.

"Can't. We're already Dungeon Lizards From Hell."

"Well, how many times do you want to be from hell?"

"No, it's just—"

"Let's play, man," said Mr. Gernsbach.

It was a good practice. The vocals were crisp (Robert's voice only cracked twice, Mr. Foster didn't lose any high notes, and Delft was merely spectacular), the horns punched. Darryl's guitar licks curled in dead-on cue around the piano, and he and Sam and Mr. Gernsbach were grinning at each other as they felt their rhythms lock into a groove. The parrot flapped around. The dog padded out and lay in the doorway. By the time they wrapped up, Mr. Foster was cheering, "We can do this, people. Oh yes, we can do this. Maple Nitro rules."

Sam, who was feeling rather sweaty at this point, was stretching, as Delft turned away from her microphone. He quickly dropped his arms in case he had sweat stains. Since the drums were set up behind her, he hadn't noticed until now that she didn't look particularly happy.

"What's the matter?"

Delft shrugged. "Nothing."

"No, come on. Is it the name?"

"No," Delft said. "I'm just kind of nervous, is all."

"You weren't before."

"I know, but just while I was singing, I started thinking what it would be like to do this in front of people. I mean, it's one thing here, in the barn . . ."

"But you've sung in front of people tons of times." Sam remembered her strutting around the stage back at the fall fair.

"No, *I* haven't." Her voice dropped. "That was Madison Dakota. There's a difference. It's like I was in disguise."

"So wear a disguise," Sam said impulsively. "Wear a wig, whatever you want.

"But everybody will know."

"So what? Listen," he said rashly, "if you're scared of looking dumb, you wear the wig, I'll wear a crash helmet."

Delft smiled. "Aw, is that ever sweet. Thanks, Sam." Sam's knees melted. He wanted to say, "Know what? Your voice is the real maple nitro," but his tongue seemed to have melted along with his knees. In the second or so it took to become vocal again, Delft turned to Amanda, and Otis flew out the door.

Chapter 35

The next afternoon, Sam went to work, finishing the raking at the Goodenoughs'. The weather had continued to be warm, and after a while Sam was happy to accept Mrs. Goodenough's offer of an iced tea.

"Earl told me you two did quite a little tag-team number there at the school board." They were standing in the driveway. Mrs. Goodenough, who was about to go out, spoke in an authoritative drawl. The drawl was no doubt partly due to the cigarettes she smoked. The ring of authority was no doubt due to having to deal with J. Earl. "Frankly, I'm amazed you liked the book. I had a look at it when I got back from Mexico." She raised a skeptical eyebrow. "I remember Earl once told me he wrote it because he needed the advance to buy a used car."

"Well," Sam said as politely as he could, "actually, I didn't say I liked it. I just said I didn't think it should be banned because it was bad."

"Aaaah," Mrs. Goodenough rumbled up a chuckle. "Another case of Earl's selective hearing. I should have known. Well, you're ahead of me, Sam. Sometimes he doesn't hear *anything* I say. Good for you, speaking your mind."

"He'd probably be pretty mad though, if he found out."

She shook her head. "Earl believes there's no such thing as bad publicity. The book got republished thanks to the kerfuffle.

Between royalties and the lecture tour, he's made out like a bandit. Laughing all the way to the bank, as Liberace used to say."

Sam drank some tea and wondered who Libberahchee was. This reminded him of another obscure personage and a question from Robin. As Mrs. Goodenough turned to walk away, he called, "Do you know if he got my sister's article about that Xavier the Savior guy?"

Mrs. Goodenough stopped short. "You mean F. Xavier Muldoon, the hockey player?"

"Yeah. He said Robin should do an article on him, so she sent him a copy. She got an A."

"Really? I'd like to see that. I've just run across his name myself, doing some reading for a project."

"Oh. 'Cause Robin found this picture that she says is J. Earl and O. Sidney Glebe with the hockey guy when they were kids, like, in Lettuceville or something."

"Cabbagetown," Mrs. Goodenough supplied. She had turned back to face Sam. "That's impossible. How old were they?"

"I don't know. Younger than me. Ten, maybe."

"TEN? Sorry," said Mrs. Goodenough. "It's just that Earl and Sid and I all met for the first time in university, after the war. I knew Earl grew up in Cabbagetown—he never shut up about it—and even took his name from Muldoon, but Sid comes from Winnipeg."

"What do you mean, his name?" Sam asked, remembering another question he was supposed to ask.

"He made it J. Earl to have the same pattern as F. Xavier."

"What does the J stand for?"

"Nothing."

"Nothing doesn't start with J."

"No, no. He has no first name that starts with J. He just added it on for the sound. His real name is Earl Patrick Goodenough, and he didn't want to switch that to P. Earl.

"Why not? Oh. Yeah, I see."

"Right," said Mrs. Goodenough. "Not what you'd call distinguished."

"But that's what O. Sidney Glebe did too," Sam exclaimed. He related the rest of his conversation with Glebe, including the reference to the black spot.

"What the hell are they up to?" Mrs. Goodenough shook her head, musing. "Of course, back then, living in Winnipeg, the Leafs still would have been his team. But . . ."

"Do you think a black spot is why they don't like each other?"

Mrs. Goodenough gave out another nicotine-tinged chuckle. "The reason they don't like each other is me. I met them through the campus arts society, and they both fell for me like a ton of bricks. As they should have. At the time I was what you would probably call a babe. I was also from Rosedale, which is a very tony neighborhood in Toronto, and I'd already published a couple of poems. They were all over themselves to impress me, and jealous of each other as all get out, to boot."

"And you married J. Earl." Sam supplied the ending.

"Oh, no. That was years later. I passed them both over for the idiot who became my first husband."

"Oh."

"Anyway, Sam, I want to see that picture."

"I'll tell Robin."

"Good." Mrs. Goodenough took out her cigarettes and paused to light up. "And I'm going to do a little more research myself, this afternoon." Then, more to herself, she said, "He always told everyone he came from Winnipeg." She blew out a cloud of smoke and strode off down the street.

Chapter 36

Sam finished his iced tea and put the glass on the back porch. After another half-hour of yard work, he mounted his bike and headed for home. His bike was a little small for him, but now that it was shorts weather, riding was permissible. No self-respecting drummer could afford to be seen wearing ankle clips.

As he labored to the top of the Princess Street hill, he spotted a familiar face. It was Mr. Gernsbach, driving slowly and looking everywhere but at the road. He was also wearing women's clothes. *Uh-oh,* thought Sam.

Their paths crossed at the stop sign. "Hi," Sam called. "What are you *doing?*" He made a vague and, he hoped, discreet gesture at his own clothing.

"Got a call somebody saw Otis over here." Mr. Gernsbach scanned the trees lining the street. "I didn't wanta take the time to change, man. Do you see him?"

Sam looked up. He'd forgotten about the missing parrot.

"There!" Mr. Gernsbach cried, his face pressed to his windshield. He leaned out the open window. "Otis, Otis!"

"Dig it," cawed the parrot. "MC5. Dig it." Sam caught a flash of yellow-green as it flapped away.

"Come on," said Mr. Gernsbach. Sam followed on his bike. They rolled slowly down the block, watching the foliage.

"Otis!"

"Otis!"

At the next stop sign, J. Earl rolled up from the opposite direction. "What's going on?" he called to Sam.

"We're trying to catch Mr. Gernsbach's parrot."

"Ah." J. Earl's eyebrows arched as he took in Mr. Gernsbach's sleeveless sundress. It made an interesting combination with the skull tattoo.

"Don't even ask, man," said Mr. Gernsbach.

Sam saw J. Earl's eye dart to a flash of movement. "There!" he pointed. Otis swooped to a backyard down the block. "Tell you what," J. Earl said. "You go this way, I'll circle the block. We'll box him in. What's his name?"

"Otis." Sam pushed off on his bike. Two doors down, Darryl, Larry, and their band mates emerged from Larry's garage, carrying skateboards.

"Whattaya doin?"

Sam explained. They followed. Since they weren't any better at skateboarding than Sam was, this didn't exactly speed the process.

"Otis!"

"Whiskey." A bush rustled. Otis emerged and plunked down on a fence. He cocked his head at them. Mr. Gernsbach got out of his car, paused to tug up the heel strap on his yellow sandals, then began a cautious approach across the lawn. Sam held his breath, in part because he'd just noticed that Mr. Gernsbach had painted his toenails. At which point the skateboarders rasped up. Larry missed his stop, rolled through the ditch, and executed a face plant into the lawn.

"Lar-ry," Steve sighed. Larry sat up sheepishly.

"Walkies," squawked Otis. "Rubber Soul." He took off into the backyard.

"Damn!" said Mr. Gernsbach.

"Know what you did there, eh?" Darryl explained to Larry. "You didn't weight-shift to—"

"Darryl, not now." Sam ran for the backyard. Otis carried on to J. Earl's side of the block. "Mr. Goodenough, he's coming!" Sam yelled and doubled back for his bike.

They circled the block and met J. Earl, who was stopped behind Smitty's pickup truck. Smitty himself was on a ladder, where he'd been taking down a client's storm windows. At the moment, though, he was slowly reaching for Otis, who was perched on the eaves trough above him. With Smitty's hand an inch away, Otis decamped lazily over the roof.

"Aw, for—" Mr. Gernsbach trotted for the backyard, hiking his shoulder straps. "Head him off. Get next door!"

Smitty started down the ladder. Darryl hopped off his skateboard and seized the gate to the yard next door. A snarl that suited a medium-sized bear sounded from the other side. Darryl let go of the gate. A frenzied volley of barking erupted. "Walkies?" they heard Otis inquire. There was more barking.

Next door, Amanda looked out from her family's kitchen. "What are you doing?"

"MC5, Purple Haze." Otis skittered upward and flapped back the way they had come, as Smitty trotted up, his aluminum extension ladder on his shoulder.

"Awwww!"

"Effff!"

"Back this way!" J. Earl was roaring from the street. Amanda grabbed her bike.

In fits and starts Otis led them all downtown. Near the Four Corners they picked up Ashley, Robin (shooting a picture of the band shell for the *Eternal),* and a group of disgruntled skids from Lint Lane. Otis had paused there, atop one of the Mozart-less speakers, and deposited mementos on the brims of two fullback ball caps below.

Now he led them back up Princess Street, pausing for a brief rest on the head of J. Earl's peeing-boy fountain, where he advised everyone to dig it. J. Earl huffed into his garage and emerged with a long-handled fishing net. He swooped in. Otis dodged. J. Earl netted the statue, swore, and wiped sweat from his shiny brow. Everyone else watched the parrot execute a lazy but not very graceful glide down the block, blip over a *For Sale* sign, and disappear behind the Doberman mansion.

"All right," said Smitty, shouldering his ladder. "He's tired. This is it."

"Right on," said Mr. Gernsbach. His ponytail had begun to fly away as well.

Mrs. Doberman's Range Rover was parked in the driveway. This, Sam felt, was not a good sign. "Spread out," J. Earl ordered as they reached it. "Quietly."

They crept across the property, gradually encircling the house in a pincer movement. Leaves rustled. Robin silently took pictures.

"I don't think we should be doing this," Sam whispered, remembering the lawn ornament adventure. Thanks to the book banning, Mrs. Doberman had caused him enough trouble already.

"Don't be a wuss, Sammy." Robin the intrepid reporter focused on Mr. Gernsbach. Sam dropped back to the rear, where two of the skids were, for unknown reasons, silently knuckle-punching each other's biceps.

Ahead, Mr. Gernsbach raised a warning hand at the corner of the mansion. Voices sounded from behind the house. Sam crept up behind Smitty and Amanda and peered through the bushes.

On the terrace beside the swimming pool sat O. Sidney Glebe, Mrs. Goodenough, and Mrs. Doberman in one of her trademark sunhats. The Dobermans' ancient golden retriever lay beside her chair, snoozing in the sunshine.

Glebe was leaning back in his chair, saying, ". . . not narrative, but texture—" Then he paused, open-mouthed, as Otis swooped down. The parrot plopped gracelessly onto Mrs. Doberman's head.

"Crawk," he said. "Walkies, Whiskey?"

The dog opened one eye as Mrs. Doberman shrieked and toppled backward into the pool.

"Dig it," said Otis, and flew to Mr. Gernsbach.

Chapter 37

"Hawlpblub!" cried Mrs. Doberman. O. Sidney Glebe and Mrs. Goodenough had jumped up as she hit the water, but now they froze as people poured from the bushes. Smitty jogged to the pool, extending one end of his ladder. Mrs. Doberman imperiously waved him away. She had made it to the pool ladder under her own steam, leaving her straw hat bobbing behind her in the deep end. It looked like a desert island, complete with nylon daisy for a palm tree.

There was total silence as she emerged from the pool, excepting the creak of the ladder and the splash of water onto the terrace stones. Her eyes widened slightly as she took in the vision that was Mr. Gernsbach and Otis, surrounded by skids, kids, Smitty, and Robin. Her eyes narrowed as she saw J. Earl.

"Get out," she said. "Now." She stalked soggily into the house.

Darryl and the boys tried a pass or two on the terrace with their skateboards as they left. Amanda borrowed a board before she got to her bike and showed them how to do it properly. The skids washed their cap brims in the pool, tried to throw each other in, then sauntered off, still punching. Smitty turned to Sam and Robin.

"Need a ride?"

Sam was about to answer when Robin hushed them.

" . . . you tell me just what's going on here, Dot," J. Earl was fuming.

Mrs. Goodenough folded her arms. "Well, Earl, since you finally seem ready to listen, I'll tell you. Again. I've been meeting a lot with Siddy because he's asked me to be the librettist for his next work. It's a kind of opera. Set in Cabbagetown in the thirties. I've written a feature role for a loudmouthed fire hydrant that comments on the passing scene. Remind you of anyone?"

J. Earl's mouth opened, but no sound came out. Mrs. Goodenough continued,

"Sid and I were just pitching the project to Felice, hoping she might be one of the sponsors. I think she might have signed on, too, for big bucks, until you barged in with the circus."

At which point O. Sidney Glebe and Mr. Gernsbach strolled over to Sam, with Otis along for the ride. Glebe had reverted to his trademark imperturbability. "Carl and I were just reminiscing about my *Bacchanal,* back in the sixties."

"Buzzard Ugly's last gig." Mr. Gernsbach nodded. "Ready for the big time when it all fell apart."

"What happened?" Robin asked.

"Ah, the usual. Guitar player went to India, drummer wanted a sex change, lead singer switched to mime. It was the sixties, eh?"

"At any rate," said Glebe, "since your new group is part of the Hope Springs soundscape, I can use them as part of the *Suite.*"

"You mean you want us to play?" Sam butted in.

"I do. I think two songs. At a precise time."

"Cool."

"Indeed."

"Rubber Soul." This was from Otis.

"I think your band—"

"Maple Nitro," Mr. Gernsbach supplied.

"Hey!" J. Earl looked around, startled.

"Exactly," Glebe continued. "Maple Nitro might lend an interesting cross-grain to the sonic texture."

"The sonic texture?" Robin's nose wrinkled.

Glebe performed his nose-pinch-to-beard-stroke move. "There will also be a string quartet, a choir, prerecorded sound"— here he glanced at Sam—"two pianos, and semi-orchestrated ambient backgrounding."

"Huh?"

Glebe smiled patiently. "Have you ever heard any of my work? I didn't think so. Yet I seem to be the only Canadian composer most people have heard of."

"Thanks to shameless self-promotion," growled J. Earl.

"Tell us about it, Earl," said his wife.

"I don't deny it." Glebe shrugged. "But you have to, to survive. You have to find sponsors for noncommercial work. And face it, Earl. We learned at the feet of a master."

"Hmpff." J. Earl scowled, but subsided.

"Anyway," Glebe went on, "most of my experimental work is unrecorded. Each performance is quite different, partly dictated by chance. I don't imagine Felice Doberman has actually heard much either."

"Lucky for you." This was from J. Earl again.

"Maybe so. You'll notice Dorothy and I were here soliciting funds *before* the premiere of *Hope Springs Suite.* Never mind. We'll find funding somewhere. I expect she would have canceled the check anyway, after she hears how I've scored the demolition derby into the ambient background."

Sam, who had been trying unsuccessfully to block out the embarrassing sounds of adult bickering, snapped to attention. "But you can't," he blurted. "She told Smitty it had to be canceled so it doesn't interfere."

Smitty nodded. "You can hear it all over town."

"Good," said Glebe. "Don't cancel it."

"Suits me," Smitty shifted his ladder. "But you'd better be careful. Mrs. D. usually gets her way."

"Yeah," Robin chimed in. "Look how she got that classical music to drive the skids out of Lint Lane."

"She did that?" Glebe sighted down his nose as if it were a rapier.

"And she almost got J. Earl's book banned, too," said Sam.

"What? *She* did that?" J. Earl's head, already pink, began to turn a darker red.

Sam gave out his second explanation of the day. When he was done, Glebe turned to J. Earl.

"I think a black spot might be in order here."

J. Earl's head darkened even further. He looked at his wife, then at Glebe. Then he nodded. "Let's talk."

"Before you do," said Mrs. Goodenough dryly, "you're both going to do some talking to me. About a photograph. Robin?"

Chapter 38

"Now remember," Mr. Carnoostie was saying, "the sound bounces around in here, so stay forward and listen to Sam for the beat. Even if it doesn't sound balanced in here, it's going to sound great out there." Standing behind his keyboard on the right side of the band-shell stage, he tugged down on his black tuxedo jacket.

"Eff," said Darryl, fumbling with his patch cord. His Telecaster was strapped on over a shapeless black suit that he had purchased, along with a porkpie hat, at the Big Sisters resale store. The ensemble made him look like a living garbage bag. Still, Sam liked this look better than last night's. Everyone, including Darryl's parents, had gone to see Dungeon Lizards From Hell with three other bands in a show at the community center. The consensus had been that the band was better than ADHD but that Darryl should never again wear either eyeliner or knee-high platform boots. Nonetheless, Sam had been jealous.

"And that's another thing," said Mr. Carnoostie, hearing Darryl swear. "This place is a natural receiver/amplifier. The sound shoots out, too, so watch what you say, even off-mike. They can hear us, we can hear them. Listen."

Sure enough, from his stool behind the drum kit, Sam could hear snatches of conversation out in the park, even the clink of bottles in the beer garden. The sun was pouring down on Canada Day. The park was bustling. Thanks to Smitty and the Yeswecans, the parade had gone off without a hitch, right down to Mr. Tompkins' fruit imitations on the Hasty Market float. At the moment, Sam could hear him taking an encore, way over by the gazebo. "An old favorite," Sam heard his voice quite clearly. "Bunch of bananas." A beat later there was a sprinkle of applause. The clarity of the sound was unnerving.

Of course, a lot of things were unnerving at this moment. Maple Nitro was only a few minutes away from its debut performance, in front of a big crowd. Sam could feel a trickle of sweat beneath his own black T-shirt as he huddled in his Survival Slouch. Black was the only dress code the band had. Everyone had adhered to it except Robert and Mr. Gernsbach. Robert, for unknown reasons, had shown up in his usual backpack, tennis shirt, and hiking shorts ensemble. Mr. Gernsbach had opted for a zebra-striped tailcoat and red-framed sunglasses, an outfit that while striking, was less controversial than the pearls and black cocktail dress he'd worn at the last rehearsal.

"Let's do it, man." Mr. Gernsbach let fall a cascade of notes from his bass. Smitty's ball cap came into view as he climbed up to the stage. Sam wiped his palms on the knees of his black jeans and looked at Delft. She was fetchingly wigless. Sam had applauded her decision to go for it, undisguised. His only regret was that her black shirt, while clingy, didn't expose her midriff the way the knotted gingham one had.

Now she looked at him nervously. Today, he'd promised himself, somehow, maybe, things would finally work out between them, leading to a perfect summer. Which only made him more nervous. Why did boy-girl things have to make you nervous instead of just being fun?

"You guys all set?" Smitty asked, approaching a microphone. Sam gave his Beatle shag a last push away from his eyes and picked up his sticks. His right leg was already bouncing to the tempo for "Midnight Hour."

"Wait," someone said. "Where's Robert?"

"Whaaaat?"

"He was here."

Everyone looked around. Sam groaned. He was *ready.* But now that he had his new tenor voice pretty much under control, Robert was the co-lead singer, with Delft. They couldn't start without him, even if he was in full nerdoid regalia. Unless his dad . . . Sam looked at his father. Mr. Foster was in a plain black shirt and jeans. He was still wearing his appalling Birkenbocker sandals, but he'd traded in his ponytail for aviator shades and a pair of sideburns Sam couldn't help but envy. His cool quotient had definitely gone up. Sam was about to throw caution to the winds and shout, "Dad, sing!"—after all, he was the guy who'd spoken his mind at the school board meeting—when Amanda said, "Here he is. Oh, *yeah!*"

Sam heard the door in the back wall of the shell open. He turned in time to see Robert walk onstage. Actually, *walk* wasn't the most accurate verb. *Strut* was closer. Or maybe *sweep.* Whatever it was, Robert had changed. He was sporting a pale blue velour tuxedo over a ruffled black shirt and neckerchief, and the biggest wrap-around mirrored shades Sam had ever seen.

"Pick it, *Wil*son," said Mr. Gernsbach appreciatively, one sharp dresser to another. Robert accepted hugs from the girls. Sam watched enviously. But then, he thought uncharitably, it didn't matter much to Robert, did it? It looked as if he'd finally come out.

"Ready?" Smitty asked again.

"Ready," said Mr. Foster.

Smitty leaned into the microphone and said, "Um, it's time for entertainment. So, uh, here's Maple Nitro." Smitty was quietly good at many things, but public speaking was not one of them. Sam sympathized. Then he rapped the rim of his snare drum, cried,

"One, two—"

He hit the two-beat stutterstep that kicked off "Midnight Hour." The horns slashed in, dead-on, then out as Mr. Gernsbach looped the signature bass riff around Sam's shuffle beat and Darryl's chopped chords. Up front Robert shot his cuffs, wrenched his mike from the stand, and started to sing.

It was somewhere between the falsetto whoop and Robert doing the splits that Sam found himself grinning. He looked around. Everyone was grinning. Mr. Carnoostie had been right: the acoustics in the band shell were awful, but the power of the music was overwhelming everything. Bottoms twitched in time. Mr. Gernsbach's head nodded reverently before the altar of soul. Mr. Foster played a phrase, did a little spin to the music, then saw Sam watching him. He shrugged a little sheepishly. Sam laughed and moved his head in a circle, meaning *do it again*. Now his dad laughed. He tapped Amanda and Bob and Vince on the shoulders and coordinated a raggedy twirl. As he did, it occurred to Sam that maybe his dad wanted to be cool for him, too. It wasn't a thought as much as a feeling. He found himself playing harder on the next few measures.

They segued flawlessly into "Respect." Robert danced back maniacally, and Delft stepped up to sing. Right away, Sam could see some of her old Madison Dakota moves coming out. Who cared? They were supposed to—she was good at this. He hit a tricky double-time fill that rolled from ride cymbal to tom, then looked out at the audience.

Out front, heads were bobbing in the beer garden. Toes were tapping as people elsewhere stood and watched. Fingers tapped the plastic arms of lawn chairs. A gaggle of little kids were dancing down front. More to the point, a gaggle of grade eleven girls began bopping beside them.

Delft's parents sat at a picnic table, Mr. Hoogstratten slapping time with one gigantic hand and holding his wife's hand with the other, a blissful grin floating above his Lincoln beard. Sam's mom boogied energetically with Ms. Broom, Mrs. Gernsbach, Darryl's mom, Mrs. Goodenough, and, astonishingly, Mrs. Goldenrod, in front of a group of slack-jawed skids. Robin darted around with her camera. She paused to give Sam a thumbs-up as the tune ended.

There was an instant of silence, as if the sound had to travel across vast reaches of the universe before being heard. Park audiences always seemed to stay a good twenty or thirty yards back from the stage; some never even got out of their cars. And they tended to be reserved in their responses. Mr. Foster had warned everyone that you judged your success in Hope Springs by how many stayed, not by how many leapt up to applaud.

But now, the distance traveled; the sound of clapping rolled back toward the stage. A nice amount of clapping, a pleasing amount. Someone even whistled. By Hope Springs standards, it was a triumph.

The skids called for "Stairway to Heaven." Mr. Carnoostie announced a ska tune, one of the new ones Sam had suggested. The grade eleven girls looked interested. The skids stayed. You couldn't do better than that, Sam thought. He grinned again and counted it off.

Chapter 39

"Anyway, he said he really liked the article and he'd pay me to do more research on Cabbagetown, because he's decided to do a book on it and his boyhood and stuff."

"So, there's another summer job." Mrs. Foster passed pizza slices to Sam and Robin, who had just finished speaking. They had ordered in tonight because Sam and his dad had to get back to the park quickly, to prepare for the *Hope Springs Suite*. "As long as you can put up with working for J. Earl."

"Does O. Sidney Glebe know?" Sam asked, before stuffing the last of his pizza slice into his mouth. "Becawth heeth doink thad hoppera, eh?" The second part came after stuffing the last of his pizza slice in his mouth. He rose from the table.

Robin shrugged. "Who knows? They're both nutbars. Smart, but nutbars."

Sam grinned around his mouthful of food. It was as good an analysis as he'd ever heard. Besides, he had a lot to grin about. After the set at the band shell, Maple Nitro had immediately been booked to play at the fall fair, Sam had gotten fifty dollars cash as his share for playing, and an invitation to do some drumming from some guys in grade eleven and twelve who were heavily into Nirvana. It looked as if Darryl wasn't going to be the only one with a side project.

A big audience had already set up its lawn chairs by the time Sam and his dad arrived. Of course, there was a bigger crowd at the demolition derby, which even now could be heard revving up across town. Looking at the general primness of the music lovers, Sam couldn't help but wonder if Maple Nitro wasn't in the wrong place. Soul didn't seem to be their thing. On the other hand, whose was it? Looks could be deceiving. Sam still hadn't quite gotten over Robert's onstage metamorphosis.

Several small stages had been built around the perimeter of the park, one for each of the wildly different musical groups taking part in the *Suite*. The two pianos had been hoisted to the band-shell stage. Mr. Foster stopped to talk to Smitty. Sam proceeded to Maple Nitro's stage, where they had set up following the afternoon show.

Darryl was already there, making infinitesimal adjustments to the controls on his Twin Reverb amp. Sam adjusted his drum kit just so.

"Hey, Sam?" Darryl's jutting ears somehow made his porkpie hat seem smaller than it was. "Know how I'm playing in Dungeon Lizards?"

"Well, yeah. I was there, remember?"

"Yeah, I know. Well, anyway, for Jeff's birthday? His dad is helping us rent this recording equipment and it's right in the middle of when Tyler is going to be away on holidays with his family and they can't change it. So we were wondering if you'd maybe like to play drums, just for that time, like, so we can still do it."

Sam was stunned. A chance to record! "Oh, wow. Yeah, thanks, Darryl."

"Cool. I'll tell the guys. 'Cause one of the tunes we want to do is 'Dragonsbreath' and you know it, so that's good. Are you doing anything after, tonight? Do you want to hang out?"

"Sure."

"Okay, 'cause I was thinking we should rent a video—"

Darryl was really only getting warmed up when Sam, glancing over the top of his ride cymbal, cut him off. "Darryl, look!"

Amanda and Robert were strolling across the park toward the stage. Robert's tux glowed, electric blue in the rays of the setting sun. This was not what had caught Sam's eye. What had done that was the fact that Robert and Amanda walked hand in hand.

They let go as they reached the stage. Robert stopped for a swig from his water bottle. Amanda brushed by Sam to open her saxophone case. Darryl's mouth still hung open. Sam whispered, "Amanda! Are you . . . is Robert, like, your . . . ?"

"Uh-huh."

"Since when?"

"Officially? Since yesterday. Since we went and rented the blue tuxedo for him. But I've known he likes me for a long time, thanks to you, partly."

"Me?"

"You told me I had a mystery admirer, remember? I started paying attention."

"Oh. Wow. Gee. Uh . . ."

"Anyway," Amanda mercifully cut him off, "it wasn't till we got the tuxedo that he told me he was the one who kissed me that time when we were doing the Christmas trees in the theater. Long time or what, huh? You guys are so dumb about not talking."

"He was the one? But isn't he, um . . ."

"No," Amanda said. "He's not. Just 'cause he sings high and dresses different doesn't mean anything. I mean, look at Mr. Gernsbach. What Robert is, is very sweet and very cute."

Cute? *Cute?* Sam and Darryl looked over at Robert. He looked like a grade eleven in a velour tuxedo, with a bad haircut and floppy hands. Granted, he was pretty much zit-free and he turned into a different person when he sang, but was this cute? No, it was not. There was no accounting for it. After all, there had been a time there when Amanda liked *him.* Sam didn't think he looked anything like Robert, and he didn't want to find out any differently. He steered the conversation to safer ground.

"Have you seen Delft?" he asked.

Amanda turned to look at him. "Haven't you seen her?"

"Not since this afternoon." Right after their set, just before the guys from the other band had come up. She'd told him how important his friendship and encouragement had been for her this year, when she'd really needed it; and how much fun she'd had. They'd chuckled over Madison Dakota, reminisced about taping for O. Sidney Glebe, laughed about her dad's misunderstandings. They'd done everything but, well—everything but sort of, you know. But that was mainly because she had to go off and meet someone. Clearly Amanda was right: it was time for talking, real talking. This did not necessarily make Sam feel good.

"Oh," said Amanda. "Well, she's around. I saw her over there, somewhere." She gestured toward the band shell. Darryl, as soon as the conversation had shifted from Robert, had already strolled off in that direction. Sam took a deep breath and headed over as the town hall clock struck eight.

At the steps leading up to the band-shell stage, he saw a group of people that included J. Earl and O. Sidney Glebe. Things would shortly be getting underway. Delft was nowhere to be seen. As he watched, the two men climbed the steps. A microphone waited at the far side of the stage. J. Earl was waving at it as they went, saying something to Glebe. Something told Sam he was trying his microphone trick again. He watched Glebe shake his head, then the two men conferred at the edge of the stage. Finally, J. Earl, clearly disgruntled, dug in his pocket and pulled out a coin, which he proceeded to flip. Glebe smiled and made an after-you gesture. J. Earl sighed and stepped to the mike.

The audience settled. A metallic screech, followed by a bang, echoed from the demolition derby. A raucous voice crackled faintly from the fairground loudspeaker. *Let's rock 'em and sock 'em boys. Rock 'em and sock 'em.*

J. Earl said, "Good evening. I'm J. Earl Goodenough," the way he always did on TV. There was applause. He went on. "Before you hear the, ah, *music* tonight, I've been asked to say a few words. A lot of people seem to think Sid Glebe grew up in Winnipeg, but in fact, we grew up together as neighbors in Cabbagetown, in Toronto. And like every kid on our street, we added an initial to our name in honor of F. Xavier Muldoon, Xavier the Savior, the greatest goalie the Leafs ever had, another Cabbagetown kid like us."

There was a sprinkling of applause from older, nostalgic hockey fans. J. Earl raised his hand. "Every year that fella would host a Christmas party for all us kids in the neighborhood. Out of his own pocket. I got my first book there: *Treasure Island*. Sid got his first musical instrument: a chromatic harmonica.

"In memory of that generosity, Sid and I have decided to do something. Along with Felice Doberman, we're going to endow and pay the liability insurance on a downtown space for kids to hang around in here in Hope Springs, which we want to call Muldoon's. There will be no piped-in Mozart. Mrs. Doberman, Sid, and I may disagree on what music is, but we share a sense of what sounds right in a neighborhood."

Here he was interrupted again by applause, which he generously accepted. He raised a well-timed hand for silence just as the clapping seemed about to die away.

"Thank you. What's right is the sound of voices, of all ages, even if they occasionally—"

He was interrupted yet again as a youthful driver burned rubber out of the parking lot behind the band shell. From somewhere near the river a boom box erupted with a thunderous triple-time beat Sam knew well. Recycled Lepers's intoxicating blend of retro, rap-metal, ska, and punk sweetened the golden evening air as a group of skids shambled across the far corner of the park, bound for no place in particular.

"This bites!" one shouted. "Where's the fireworks?"

J. Earl visibly wrestled his blood pressure back down to sub-stroke level.

"—even if they occasionally *offend,*" he continued. "Ladies and Gentlemen, O. Sidney Glebe."

Chapter 40

J. Earl stepped back from the mike. Glebe cocked his head at the band shell for a moment, then ambled to a spot between the two pianos. When the applause died away, he began to speak.

"Thank you, Earl, and thank *you,* too, for your support and for this town."

Glebe's voice was perfectly, eerily audible without the microphone. Outwitted at his own game, J. Earl glared.

"Hope Springs is a place whose depth and diversity can easily be missed," Glebe went on. "Day to day we accept its surface too easily. We forget what's underneath."

It seemed to Sam that something was missing from what he was hearing. Then he realized he'd been half-expecting Darryl to recap Mr. Carnoostie's explanation of the acoustical properties of the band shell. Except Darryl, he now saw, was some yards away, chatting with a girl in a headband, apparently about a guitar she was carrying. He had a sudden intuition that maybe he and Darryl wouldn't be getting together later after all. What else was new?

Meanwhile, Glebe was saying, "What you will hear is my impression of a year in the life of the town. Some of it may be sacred, some profane"—Sam's head snapped back around, tugged by an unwelcome memory of them all swearing into the tape player. He had erased that, hadn't he? *Hadn't* he?—"but it all comes from here, and from you. Some months ago, at the high school, we discussed what music is and whether listeners help to create it. At the time, I reminded the students that, in the Bible, the sound of God's voice comes even before the light. Of course, with Earl here, that is sometimes true as well."

The line got a bigger laugh here than it had at school. Sam watched J. Earl pretend to chuckle politely. Glebe said, "When we were kids, Earl played a trick on me. The year after he got his book and I got my harmonica, he left an anonymous note for me on my porch at Halloween. It said, *Leave all your candy here or the black spot will get you.* I was a year younger, but I knew my pirates. I left out my candy, and I was terrified for months. Hope Springs reminded me of that for the first time in years—and also helped me let it go."

"That means they black-spotted Felice Doberman." Sam smelled cigarette smoke. He turned to see Mrs. Goodenough.

"Huh?"

"Blackmail," she chuckled throatily. "The boys told her that if she didn't kill the music in Lint Lane and kick in for a teen space, they'd buy that property for sale across from her and open a drop-in center. The choice was downtown or her front yard."

"Wow." Sam was genuinely impressed.

"Oh, they play hardball."

"So does that mean they're friends now?"

She chuckled again. "Not exactly. You know, I think Earl felt so guilty about that spot trick that he's disliked Siddy ever since."

Sam made an uncomprehending face.

"The way Earl sometimes thinks," Mrs. Goodenough tried to explain, "it would have been Sid's fault for making him feel so badly."

Sam tried to wrap his brain around that one. Mrs. Goodenough drew on her cigarette, then smiled as she exhaled. "It makes sense and it doesn't," she admitted. "It's the same reason Earl never ratted on Siddy's not being from Winnipeg. He would have had to admit they'd grown up together, and he didn't want anything to do with him. Which is too damn bad, for both of them. Forgive and forget is not a bad motto, Sam."

Sam nodded. Adults were clearly a whole other species. Or were they? He watched Darryl hurry past in his garbage-bag suit, whispering animatedly to the girl and making sure not to look in Sam's direction.

From the stage, Glebe's mild tones floated out to them.

"I'm delighted," he was saying, "that you have come to listen. It's part of creating. Life, like a black spot, can be surprising, even frightening, but that's part of what makes it worthwhile. The sounds you hear tonight may not always be what you're expecting, but that is part of creation too.

"I wish to thank all the musicians contributing here this evening, including yourselves," he gestured to the audience, "and a young man named Sam Foster, who, with his colleagues, devoted much time and effort to taping material for me, as well as helping me understand some things. Finally, I wish to thank Mrs. Felice Doberman, a most generous patron of the arts.

"We have some final preparations to make, and the *Suite* will commence in exactly . . . twelve minutes. Thank you."

Sam turned and floated back toward Maple Nitro's stage. Half of him was silently crying out, *that was meee he was talking about,* but he noticed the other half had already dropped him into his old Survival Slouch, something he'd used less of lately. He was halfway back when he heard a voice.

"Sam."

He turned. It was Delft. *"Hi."*

"Hi." It wasn't just the pinkening sky. She was blushing.

Delft said, "That was really nice the way he thanked you."

"He thanked all of us."

"Well, you deserved it the most."

Sam pushed back his hair to hide his embarrassment. "Well, you helped too. Like we were saying before, about when we went around taping." *Say something else,* a voice inside was screaming. *This is it! Don't be a wuss! Invite her somewhere! Ask if she wants to do something after! Go for it, you're the guy who's brave enough to talk!* Sam opened his mouth. This was harder than town council, harder than the school board. "And, um, maybe would you, like—"

"Listen," Delft interrupted, a little too brightly, "I want you to meet my friend, Henk. Sam, this is Henk. Henk, this is Sam."

For the first time, Sam realized there was a boy standing behind her. He was unfamiliar, shorter than Sam, but sturdier. And older. That was all he took in, because he'd suddenly understood what *friend* meant: boyfriend. Delft had a boyfriend. She was saying, "Henk's been in Holland all year on a student exchange. Now he's back."

"Oh," he managed. Henk was wearing a light blue shirt. About the color of an airmail envelope. "Cool. Hi. Well, I have to go get ready."

It was Survival Slouch all the way. Amanda gave him a sympathetic look over her saxophone as he slipped onto his drum stool.

"I thought maybe she'd already told you," she said. "I know she wanted to. If it helps, I think she didn't because she liked you too much."

"It doesn't matter."

It did, of course, but not exactly in the way Amanda thought. It hit him with the speed of the freight train that would shortly arrive. True, he'd spent the whole school year mooning, first over a girl who didn't really exist and then over a girl who already had a boyfriend. True, this seemed a waste. True, he was feeling disappointed. So why was he also feeling something like relief? He picked up his sticks and played a light, two-beat fill. Was it just because he'd been scared to ask her out? No. He *had* asked her to do things, and he'd talked to Delft, lots of times. Maybe he just wasn't ready to . . . to settle down. Maybe this was just a dress rehearsal, a getting ready to be ready. What the heck. He'd had some fun. He hadn't done anything *too* stupid. He was in two bands, with friends. Grade eleven girls had danced to the beat he'd helped put down. He'd survived grade nine. Summer was waiting. He was free.

Darryl climbed aboard and strapped on his guitar. "So what movie do you want to rent?" he asked.

Sam, shaken from his reverie, could only blink. What had happened to—what did it matter? Forget. Forgive. Live. He shrugged. "Anything." As he said it, he could feel the Survival Slouch dropping away. *Free.* There was the incredible, dislocating sensation of being himself. Something inside of him began to soar, a feeling so pure you could only have it at fourteen.

Somewhere below him things were happening. On his bed at home, a breath of air through the open window riffled *War and Peace,* his current reading, where it lay open, beside his guitar, to page 258 (of 1,146; the number still made him shudder). Ignoring this disturbance, Prince Andrey remained on his back on the battlefield at Austerlitz, all the way onto page 259, entranced by the peacefulness of clouds drifting across the sky. In the park, people were still arriving. On the stage, the rest of the band was gathering itself.

"Three minutes," said Mr. Carnoostie, checking his watch.

"Dig it," said Mr. Gernsbach.

The performance would begin as the 8:22 freight rumbled across the viaduct. Floating in his own private sky, Sam listened to Hope Springs. Across town, the demolition derby screeched and banged. Leaves stirred in a warm evening breeze. Laughter mixed with the murmur of voices. Lawn chairs clanked. A bass note sounded. The string quartet found their A. A car rolled by, then a skateboard. He breathed. And from far off in the distance came the endless whisper of traffic on the highway, bound for the rest of Sam's life.

It was music to his ears.

Ted Staunton's witty and keen-eyed observations of the behavior of kids and adults make *Sounding Off* an absorbing and thoroughly entertaining read. His previous books include the well-loved Cyril and Maggie series, the Morgan series and *Puddleman* (Red Deer Press, 1999). His Monkey Mountain series (Red Deer Press and *Hope Springs a Leak* (Red Deer Press, 1998), the precursor to *Sounding Off*, were his first looks at life in the fictional town of Hope Springs.

He has received numerous Canadian Children's Book Centre Our Choice Citations, as well as Silver Birch Award and Hackmatack Award nominations for *Hope Springs a Leak*.